Harmony of the Witch

Crypt Witch cozy paranormal mystery series - book 9

K.E. O'Connor

K.E. O'Connor Books

HARMONY OF THE WITCH

Copyright © 2022 by K.E. O'Connor

ISBN: 978-1-915378-07-1

Written by: K.E. O'Connor

Chapter 1

"Oops! Sorry." A tipsy witch almost spilled her lemon drop down my favorite sparkly black top as she staggered past on crazily high heels.

I stepped back and bumped into a warlock. Cloven Hoof was full to bursting tonight, and the only person I could blame for that was Granny Dottie and how ridiculously popular she was in Willow Tree Falls.

Every member of my family was here, along with most of the village and a huge group of Granny Dottie's friends. We were celebrating her turning sixty-nine. Although I was pretty certain she'd been celebrating being sixty-nine for at least five years.

Merrie and Paula rushed past me with trays full of lemon drops, bubbling champagne witch brew, and ginger ice mojitos, ensuring everyone was supplied with drinks.

My chef, Niall, was cooking up a storm in the kitchen, producing an endless supply of tasty nibbles for the dancing, laughing, and mainly drunken crowd of partygoers.

Wiggles bounced past, sporting a jaunty red bowtie, his tail wagging as he socialized. He was always the extravert.

Skulking behind him was Bandit, her ginger tail down and her ears lowered. It looked like noisy crowds and loud music weren't her thing.

I stood with my back against the wall as the music throbbed through me, keeping an eye on things and trying to keep my mind off the subject that had been front and center of my thoughts for what felt like months.

I was still no closer to finding my missing dad. And since I'd now involved Aurora and Granny Dottie in finding out what had happened to him, it wouldn't be long before the secret spread through the village. Aurora was terrible at keeping secrets, and Granny Dottie often let slip things she shouldn't. Once word got out, it would be chaos. Everyone would offer help or words of caution.

A hand wrapped around my waist. I looked up and smiled as Rhett Blackthorn leaned against the wall next to me.

"Hey, Tempest. Are you enjoying the party?" He lightly kissed my lips.

"So long as everyone else is having a good time, that's the main thing." I leaned against him, enjoying the familiar scent of bike oil and citrus cologne.

He squeezed me tighter. "You too. This may be your club, but you should let your hair down as well."

"I can let my hair down just fine. You know that."

"I sure do." Rhett was quiet for a moment. Quiet was his default mode, but I sensed something coming. "What's on your mind?"

And there it was. "The usual."

His soft grunt told me he didn't believe me, but he never pushed. That was one of the many things I loved about being in a relationship with Rhett. That and he was so easy on the eyes and fun to hang out with. A sexy fallen angel in leather, and he was all mine.

I'd yet to confide in him about my dad. I didn't want to waste people's time or get their hopes up that Dad was coming back. I could be searching for someone who was no longer alive. Although that thought made me sick, so I never dwelled on it. The rare sightings of Dad could simply be a mistake.

That was the main reason I'd kept this to myself and only shared it with a couple of people. And if I told Rhett, he'd get involved. He'd enlist his biker gang to start the hunt.

Maybe I was being a coward for not getting more people entangled in this, but what if that hunt revealed an answer I didn't want to hear? What if Dad really was nothing more than a ghost?

"Your granny's having fun," he said.

Granny Dottie was in the middle of the dance floor shooting sparks of silver from her fingertips. People stood around her in a circle and clapped her on.

"Anyone would think she was sixteen not sixty-nine," I said. "I hope I age that well."

"You'll be a beautiful older woman," he said. "It's something I'm looking forward to seeing."

I arched an eyebrow. "You're planning on sticking around that long?"

"As long as you'll have me."

A warm glow filled my chest. We weren't an emotive couple, but Rhett was loyal, and I could always rely on him. I should let him in more. I could certainly use more people on my side in the search for my dad.

Axel Shadowsoul strode through the main doors of Cloven Hoof, drawing the attention of several women, who eyed him eagerly as he stood there looking like he owned the place. That guy was never short on self-confidence.

But he didn't notice all the admiring glances. Axel only had eyes for my bar manager, Merrie Noble. He strode over, took the tray she held and placed it on a table, swept her off her feet, and pressed a lingering kiss to her lips.

I shook my head. Axel had always been a charmer and a ladies' man. But since he'd gotten together with Merrie, he'd been devoted to her. It was sweet, but I kept an eye on him, not certain he'd changed for good. If I ever caught him cheating, I'd curse him to a long miserable life as I chased him out of Willow Tree Falls, shooting fireballs at his head.

"I see Dottie extended the party invitation to everyone in the village." Rhett scowled at Axel.

"Axel's a friend. It's fine that he's here. Besides, I thought you two were getting along."

"We get along just fine when he's not using that smart mouth of his," Rhett said. "Ever since he had his little vacation with his father, he's gotten cocky."

"He's always been cocky."

Axel set Merrie back on her feet before walking over to Granny Dottie. He planted a kiss on her cheek and presented her with a huge wrapped gift that appeared out of nowhere.

Granny Dottie giggled in delight before handing the gift over to Aurora, who was dancing next to her. She dragged Axel into the circle of excited guests to dance.

"I'll go get some drinks," Rhett said. He strolled to the bar, and I took a moment to enjoy the view. He was a picture of leather-clad perfection. Rhett had a tough side, but when you got to know him, he was a softie.

"Psst! Tempest!"

My gaze shifted as Granny Dottie staggered toward me.

"Are you enjoying yourself on the dance floor?" I caught hold of her elbow as she swayed, her cheeks glowing pink and her teased hair glittering with sparkly spray. Yeah, I so wanted to age like her.

"I needed to get you on your own." She leaned forward and spoke in my ear. "As soon as I saw that gorgeous hunk of yours disappear, I had to grab my chance."

"He's only at the bar," I said. "What do you want to talk about?"

She glanced around. "Any more thoughts on your dad?"

I grimaced. Despite grilling Granny Dottie for hours over her involvement with my dad's disappearance, and any deal made involving my incumbent demon, Frank, she'd denied any knowledge. In fact, she'd been shocked when I suggested she had something to do with Dad's disappearance.

"Nothing new. I keep hitting brick walls. I was thinking about taking a trip to the Dark Realm, see if I can dig anything up." It was the last place any magic user wanted to go unless they had something seriously bad to hide from.

"Noooo!" Granny Dottie hiccupped. "Don't go there. It's a bad place."

"It's the last place Dad was seen," I said.

"If you go there, I'm coming too." She jabbed a finger into my chest, and a tiny sparkle of silver magic shot out.

I shook my head. There was no way I was taking Granny Dottie into a place like that. She was a powerful witch, but she was also my gran. I wasn't putting her at risk. "It's just one option I'm considering. I haven't made a decision just yet."

"We'll figure this out, my girl. If he's out there, we'll find him. He can't hide forever." Granny Dottie adjusted the slightly too tight sparkly purple dress she wore and pursed her lips. "It's just that..." She glanced at the crowd of dancing partygoers.

"Go on, what do you want to say?"

"I don't want you getting your hopes up. Your information sources aren't reliable. A dark magic user and an unscrupulous rogue who makes his money stealing from others. You can't trust them. You can't trust the information."

She had an annoyingly valid point, and it had niggled away in the back of my mind ever since I'd gotten a whisper that Dad was still alive. My two sources of information regarding my dad, Foxglove

Shadowsoul and Isaac Dubrov, were less than ideal, but now I had the idea in my head that Dad might be alive, I couldn't let it go.

"I need to get this confirmed one way or the other," I said.

She patted my cheek. "We do all right, though, don't we? We've been good since he vanished. I'd hate to think you missed out on anything important because your dad wasn't around. Your mom would be devastated if she thought you were unhappy. So would I."

"No! I'm definitely not unhappy. And I didn't miss out. Sure, I missed him; we all did. But I didn't have a bad childhood because he wasn't around." I gripped her elbow. "Don't mention this to Mom. She doesn't need to know just yet. It won't do her any good to worry about this until I know for sure where he is and what sort of mess he's in."

"She won't hear it from me." Granny Dottie pressed a kiss to my cheek.

"Come on, beautiful." Axel appeared next to Granny Dottie and winked at me. "Let's get you back on that dance floor. Your adoring fans are waiting."

"You cheeky boy." She grabbed his hand and planted a sloppy kiss on his lips. "Lead the way."

I chuckled as Axel spun Granny Dottie expertly around the floor, although I wasn't sure who was leading who in the dance. Granny Dottie loved to be in charge.

My sister, Aurora, hurried over, her blonde hair piled on her head and curls drifting around her face. "Does Granny Dottie know about her big surprise?"

I shook my head. "Not unless you've told her. You haven't, I hope?"

"I've not said a word." She bounced in her glittery peep toe shoes. "It's caused me physical pain to keep this secret quiet. It's going to be amazing."

"And she's definitely coming?" Aurora had planned an elaborate musical evening led by none other than legendary singer Bathsheba Delaware, famous for her magic laced opera performances. She'd sold out all over the world when she was younger. She was semi-retired these days but still put on the occasional intimate gig.

When Aurora had suggested we get Bathsheba to come to Willow Tree Falls, I was reluctant. Why would she want to come here?

Still, Aurora was determined, and after numerous messages back and forth, Bathsheba had agreed to come. She wasn't cheap, though, and had numerous conditions before she would perform. One of which was to showcase her new music next to the stone circle in the village, using it as a stunning backdrop.

"I can't wait to meet her," Aurora said. "I haven't actually spoken to her directly. I've been dealing with her assistant, Charlotte. I think she's Bathsheba's daughter. Anyway, that doesn't matter. Everything's in place. They're arriving tomorrow and setting up at the stone circle at four o'clock."

"I've got to admit it's a great location for a concert," I said.

"I think that's what persuaded Bathsheba to come," Aurora said. "Those old stones have power."

I nodded. The stone circle in Willow Tree Falls absorbed and distributed magical energy throughout the village. It was a big draw to magic users, helping to keep everyone's energy flowing and their magic strong and stable.

"We'll have to be extra careful to keep Granny Dottie out of the way tomorrow. If she gets so much as a sniff of something strange going on, she'll investigate and ruin the surprise," Aurora said.

"I've already checked. She's on duty in the cemetery from noon until nine o'clock. Mom gave her a later shift since she figured she might need a lie-in after tonight. We'll be able to sneak in Bathsheba and her entourage when Granny's monitoring the demons. She won't see anything. By the time everything's set up, we can bring her from the cemetery straight to the stone circle."

Aurora bounced on her toes again. "I can't wait. This'll be a birthday surprise she'll never forget."

"That's the plan," I said. "You don't turn sixty-nine for the fifth time in a row and forget about it in a hurry."

Aurora laughed. "That's so true. Come on. Let's go for a boogie."

I allowed her to drag me onto the dancefloor and lost myself in the throbbing bass and lively rhythms. Rhett joined us, along with a gaggle of other friends.

I pushed my worries about my dad to one side for the night. This was an evening of celebration, a night to enjoy being with the family I still had in my life.

I'd worry about my missing dad tomorrow.

Chapter 2

"She's late!" Aurora fanned her face with her hands and stared at the magic barrier separating Willow Tree Falls from the rest of the world.

Bandit, her sassy ginger familiar, was curled in a ball on a soft patch of moss, ignoring everyone. Her mood hadn't improved since last night.

"Only by half an hour," I said. "Isn't it usual that creative types are notoriously bad at time-keeping?" I lounged against a tree, Wiggles by my side, as we waited for Bathsheba and her entourage to appear.

"We need time to set up at the stone circle," Aurora said.

Bandit sighed and lifted her nose, which had been tucked in her tail. "She's not coming."

"Don't be such a meanie," Aurora said. "You've been grumpy all day."

"She's hung over," Wiggles said. "I caught her licking the bottom of people's glasses at the club last night."

"That's disgusting." Aurora frowned at Bandit. "Is that true?"

"Of course, it's not true," Bandit said. "I don't feel very well." She tucked her nose back in her tail and closed her eyes.

"Then you ate too much party food," Wiggles said.

"That's your hobby," Bandit muttered through her fur.

Aurora ran her hands over Bandit several times. "You feel warmer than usual. Maybe you are coming down with something."

"I'm telling you it's too much drink, too much food, or she's faking it to get attention," Wiggles said.

"It's none of those things," Bandit muttered. "Haven't you got some trash you need to root around in?"

"All the trash cans have been carefully monitored," Wiggles said. "I missed nothing."

Aurora grabbed my arm as the magic barrier in front of us shifted. It shimmered like a mirage for several seconds before a large, plump woman dressed head to toe in cream silk emerged. Her long red hair flowed down her back, and she wore pearls around her neck and wrists, along with several large rings studded with jewels on her fingers. I recognized her immediately as Bathsheba.

Following right behind her was a stunning dark-haired guy in an expensive suit. He was model gorgeous. I did my best not to stare, but wowsers, he was smokin'.

He was closely followed by a striking looking pale woman with long blonde hair and enormous blue eyes. Right beside her was a short squat guy in an ill-fitting suit, with dark dreadlocks.

Aurora glanced at me and grinned before she hurried over. "Bathsheba Delaware?" She extended a hand.

The woman with red hair lifted her chin but didn't take Aurora's hand. "Of course."

"It's lovely to meet you. I'm Aurora Crypt."

The slender blonde woman stepped forward and shook her hand. "It's nice to meet you, Miss Crypt. We've been corresponding. I'm Charlotte Delaware."

"Oh! Of course." Aurora smiled brightly. "We're so happy to have Bathsheba with us today."

Bathsheba's sharp gaze drifted around, her nose wrinkling as if she smelled something unpleasant. "So, this is Willow Tree Falls? So much goes on here. And you have the stone circle. I trust I'll be performing by it as instructed?"

"Of course," Aurora said. "It's all been arranged. The stones will be delighted to welcome you."

"Yes, I'm intrigued to get a taste of their powers." Bathsheba waved the gorgeous guy in the suit closer. "Be a sweetheart and organize me a triple Frappuccino with non-fat milk and a chocolate straw. And rustle up some food. I'm starving after our journey."

"Of course, my love." He nodded at Aurora. "Is there anywhere you can recommend? My wife has exacting tastes when it comes to her food."

"Sprinkles is great," Aurora said. "You can't beat the cakes there."

"Unicorn's Trough is better for coffee." I stepped forward. "I'm Tempest Crypt, Aurora's sister."

Bathsheba's eyes narrowed for a second. "Very good. Off you go. See what you can find." She sighed as she turned her attention back to us. "The only reason I keep Liam around is because he's so easy on the eye. He's husband number four."

"Wow! That's... interesting. So many husbands." Aurora glanced at me.

Bathsheba flicked her fingers at the silent young man with the dreadlocks. "Don't stand there like a piece of wood. You've already met my daughter, Charlotte. This is my son, Picasso. They travel everywhere with me when I perform."

I nodded at Picasso, who kept his gaze on the ground, his shoulders hunched, and a large black backpack swamping him.

There were a few seconds of awkward silence.

Bathsheba sighed again. "That's what a private education gets you. Sullenness and silence."

"Shall I show you the stone circle?" Aurora asked. "I understand you've brought your own accommodation rather than staying in the hotel."

"That's correct," Bathsheba said. "I don't sleep in a bed that anyone else has used."

"What do you sleep in?" I asked.

"Picasso erects our accommodation wherever we travel. It has everything I need. I shall locate the hospitality suite by the stone circle."

"Hospitality suite?" My forehead furrowed. "You mean, a tent?"

Bathsheba smirked. "No, I do not."

"Oh! We don't normally have people stay by the stones," Aurora said. "The stone circle can be temperamental. It takes them a while to warm to strangers."

"I'm sure I can handle a simple stone circle," Bathsheba said. "I'm not without my own ability, as you will see when I perform later."

Aurora bit her bottom lip. "I'm sure everything will work out. Our granny will be thrilled that you're in Willow Tree Falls. This is the perfect birthday gift for her."

"Of course, it is." Bathsheba waved a hand in the air. "How far is this stone circle?"

"From here, it's about a twenty-minute walk," I said.

"That's too far. Picasso, transport us to the location." Bathsheba extended a hand.

"It's a nice walk," Aurora said. "You'll be able to see all the village if we go by foot. We have some great stores here. I have a store that sells—"

"I'm sure your store is delightful," Bathsheba said, "but I don't walk anywhere. Picasso, transport me to the stone circle immediately."

He stepped forward, grabbed hold of her hand, and they vanished.

"Oh!" Aurora blinked. "That was..." She looked at me and shrugged.

"Rude," I offered up.

Charlotte sighed. "Try not to take offense. Mom, I mean, Bathsheba, can be a bit... difficult. She still remembers when everywhere she went people adored her. She used to sell out in arenas and get taken first class around the world by rich men who fawned over her beauty and her singing ability."

"She's not so beautiful anymore," Bandit muttered from her curled-up position.

Charlotte stared at her for a second. "Well, we all get old. And she does have a rather sweet tooth. It makes it hard to lose weight and keep it off."

"I can sympathize," Wiggles said. "I'm always being told to keep an eye on my waistline."

"And you never listen," Bandit said.

"Goodness! Do all the animals around here talk?" Charlotte asked.

"Only a few," I said. "This is Wiggles, and the grumpy cat is Bandit."

"I don't like screechy female singers," Bandit said. "I'll stay at home this evening."

"You must come," Aurora said. "You don't want to miss out on all the fun."

"I'm sure I'll survive."

My eyebrows lifted. Bandit was usually full of sass, but she was in a truly foul mood today.

"Should we go after Bathsheba?" Aurora asked Charlotte. "I want to make sure she has everything she needs."

"Don't worry about that. She'll have everything she needs. She always does." Charlotte shook her head. "Liam runs around at her beck and call, getting her everything she demands. Picasso's on hand to transport her wherever she needs to go and make sure she's comfortable. And I, well, I do everything else."

"You and your brother don't look very much alike," I said.

"We're the total opposite," Charlotte said. "But he's the best brother. We're not actually related.

Bathsheba adopted us. She always said she didn't want children of her own in case they ruined her figure."

"What figure?" Bandit said.

Charlotte bit her bottom lip. "Bathsheba has gained a little weight recently. She used to have enviable curves. Still, a rubenesque figure is attractive to many men. She gets lots of attention wherever she goes."

"Is that because she's blisteringly rich?" I asked.

"Tempest!" Aurora swatted my arm.

Charlotte winced. "It may have something to do with it."

I shrugged. She certainly didn't get the attention because of her charming manners. "How old were you when Bathsheba adopted you?"

"We were five years old. We've been with her ever since," Charlotte said.

"It's nice she was able to give you a loving home," Aurora said. "Many children in care aren't that fortunate."

"It's been an interesting life," Charlotte said. "I've traveled the world with Mom. Now I'm older, I work as her personal assistant. I do the bookings and make arrangements for events such as this. We don't do large gigs anymore. She finds those too tiring. But places like this, she usually enjoys. Ignore her if she complains about everything. That's just her way."

"We definitely will," I said.

"Is your support act not traveling with you?" Aurora asked.

"Oh, no. Fanny and Mom never travel together. It doesn't end well when they do. She should be along soon. Fanny has all the details." Charlotte looked around. "If you don't mind, I need to head to the stone circle. Mom doesn't like being unattended for long."

"Of course. If you need anything, just let me know," Aurora said.

"Thanks. Will do."

Liam returned with a large white cake box in his hand and a tray of takeout coffees balanced on top. He looked around, and his eyes tightened. "She's already gone?"

"You know Mom doesn't like to stand for long," Charlotte said. "How about we walk through the village like you suggested, Aurora? I'd love to see the place."

"Of course," she said. "Come on, Bandit. Let's show them around."

"I can't walk. I don't have any energy." Bandit kept her eyes shut as she spoke.

"You can walk, you lazy old thing! We have to go." Aurora gently nudged Bandit with a finger.

"Prod me again and I'll bite you," Bandit said.

"I can't leave you here," Aurora said. "Someone might tread on you when they come through the magic barrier."

"I can get her to move." Wiggles stalked over. "A blast of fire should get her furry butt shifting."

"You'll regret it if you do, hound." Bandit buried her nose deeper into the fur on her tail.

"Very well! I'll carry you." Aurora scooped up Bandit and placed her in the large shoulder purse she carried for just this purpose. "Sorry about that, Charlotte. My familiar has diva tendencies."

Charlotte chuckled. "Don't worry. I know all about that."

"It'll be my pleasure to show you around. Willow Tree Falls is a lovely place to live."

"I'm certain it is." Charlotte walked alongside Aurora. "As soon as I got the invitation, I worked hard to convince Mom she had to come here. There's so much history surrounding this place."

I walked alongside Liam, who stared straight ahead, a line between his pinched brows.

"Have you been married to Bathsheba for long?" I asked.

"Eighteen months," he said.

"It must take some getting used to, being married to someone so famous. I bet you don't get a moment to yourselves."

He was silent for a second. "You could say that. It can be... trying on the relationship."

"You don't mind running about after her, fetching and carrying?"

He slid a glance my way. "She's my wife. Of course, I'm going to take care of her."

"Have you got any cakes going spare in that box?" Wiggles asked.

"These are all for Bathsheba." Liam balanced the box of cakes and coffees in one hand and slid a pair of sunglasses over his stunning blue eyes. "She gets hungry before a performance."

"She must be eating her feelings with all that cake," Wiggles said. "I do it all the time."

"What feelings are you eating?" I asked.

"I worry about you constantly," Wiggles said. "I need to eat at least one doughnut a day to keep calm."

"Your selflessness is admirable," I said. I considered trying to engage Liam in more conversation, but he clearly wasn't interested. Instead, I half-listened to Aurora as she extolled the wonders of Willow Tree Falls to Charlotte.

We reached the stone circle, and my eyes widened at the appearance of an enormous crimson patchwork Arabian style tent next to the stones.

"I wasn't expecting that." Aurora stared open-mouthed at the tent. "I mean, it's beautiful but..."

"Way too big for one person," I said.

"Mom never does anything on a small scale," Charlotte said. "And we all stay in here."

"Even so, there must be a dozen rooms," Aurora said.

"Fifteen, actually. This is Picasso's speciality. He's amazing at transportation magic and can turn his hand to anything that needs building. He had the equipment for the hospitality suite in his backpack. With a little help from a few spells, he can have the whole thing up in less than ten minutes."

"No, no, no!" Bathsheba stomped out of the rippling scarlet tent. "I need the goose down duvet. How am I expected to sleep under a poor-quality cashmere blanket and an eiderdown?"

Picasso hurried out after her, his cheeks pale. "Sorry. It was a simple mistake. I must have forgotten to pack it. I'll go find another one."

"It won't be the same." Bathsheba wheeled and jabbed a finger at him. "I won't be able to sleep under anything else. You'll have to go back and get it."

Charlotte glanced at us before hurrying over. "I'm sure we can find something that will be a suitable replacement. We'll make sure you have the perfect night of sleep."

Bathsheba scowled at her. "You can't guarantee that. This foolish boy has ruined everything. I need all my things in the right place. Otherwise, I might not be able to perform properly."

"It's just a duvet," Wiggles muttered. "What's the big deal?"

I nodded. Bathsheba was living up to the reputation of being a musical diva. It wasn't a pretty sight.

Bathsheba threw her hands up and turned away from Picasso. "I wonder why I bother with you. You cause me nothing but stress. I need calm and competency in my life before a performance, not this chaos." She flicked a hand at Liam, and he hurried over.

She grabbed a coffee from the tray, threw off the lid and drank it down. She flipped open the box of cakes, pulled out an iced pink sugared doughnut, and sunk her teeth into it.

"He's got doughnuts from Sprinkles." Wiggles dropped to his belly and inched closer.

I grabbed him around the middle. "Not so fast. Bathsheba will throttle you if you steal a doughnut."

"Just one. That box is huge."

I lifted him off the ground. "Nope, not this time. This lady has the serious grumps. She's in a worse mood than Bandit."

Wiggles grumbled to himself for a few seconds before flipping his paws over my shoulder and drooling on my hair. "Then we need to get our own cakes later. It's either that or I start stalking Liam. I need doughnuts."

"Deal. This evening has to go smoothly, so everything is perfect for Granny Dottie. And I get the impression it'll only take something small to make Bathsheba explode."

Charlotte talked quietly to Bathsheba for several minutes as she chomped her way through two more doughnuts.

"Are you sure about this?" I whispered to Aurora, who came and stood beside me. "Bathsheba takes being high maintenance to another level."

"It'll all be worth it," she said, a worried look on her face. "Just imagine Granny Dottie when she comes to the stone circle and sees her favorite performer waiting for her."

"It had better be worth it," I said. Even Frank was being stirred up by Bathsheba's rudeness, and he'd been quiet for a long time.

He was still holding out on me in regard to any deal he might have made with my dad. He hadn't made an appearance since I'd learned that something had gone down between them.

"Is this the right place?"

I turned and spotted a voluptuous middle-aged woman with jet black curls striding up the hill toward us. She had beautiful copper skin and dark, almond-shaped eyes. She was tiny, standing at just under five feet tall, even in heels.

"If you're looking for the stone circle, then you're in the right place," I said.

She puffed out a breath and grinned, her teeth a brilliant white. "I am. I'm Fanny Flotella. I'm performing with Bathsheba this evening."

"Of course." Aurora hurried over to her. "It's so nice to meet you. I'm Aurora Crypt."

Fanny hugged her. "You've been so kind giving me all the details about the event. I've been trying to get the information from Bathsheba for weeks, but she kept giving me the brush-off. She even said I shouldn't bother turning up because she didn't need a warmup act."

"Oh, no! We definitely want you here. My Granny Dottie loves your music too." Aurora led Fanny over to me. "This is my sister, Tempest."

I adjusted my grip on Wiggles and shook hands with her. "Nice to meet you."

"You too. This is so exciting." Fanny looked at the stones. "When I heard we'd be performing at the stone circle in Willow Tree Falls, I nearly fell off my seat. What a treat."

As if the stone circle had heard her praise, a spark of red light shot from one stone to the other, bouncing around the inside before flaring out in a dramatic sparkle of glitter.

I grinned. "Our stones are happy to have you here."

Fanny clapped her hands together. "Do they always do that? Wouldn't it be magnificent if I was singing, and the stones performed along with me?"

Another shower of sparkly magic shot from the top of the stone circle.

"You can never predict what the stone circle will do," I said. "From the looks of things, they're set to entertain us all tonight."

Fanny's bright smile faded when she saw Bathsheba. "I see her Highness is already here. How much trouble has she caused?"

"She's been a real pain in the—"

"Bathsheba's been fine." Aurora cut me off. "She's just settling in. We've had a few bumps along the way, but I'm sure, once you're both warmed up, everything will be fine."

"I doubt that's true," Fanny said quietly. "I rarely perform alongside Bathsheba these days. Our rivalry has grown over the years. As her ability has faded, mine has grown. She hates that."

"You don't get along?" I asked.

"To begin with, we got along okay. She's older than me, and when we first met, I considered her a mentor. Then her star became stellar, and she lost touch with reality. She thinks everyone should grovel on their knees around her. I'm not denying she has a good voice; well, she used to have an incredible voice, but not so much anymore. I don't like to blow my own horn, but I should be headlining these days. Bathsheba's washed up, and she knows it."

"She still has a beautiful voice," Aurora said. "I heard her live performance at the Godiva Concert Hall a few months ago."

Fanny arched an eyebrow. "We can all sound incredible when we use the right... enhancements.

Each performance I give is natural and unique. Just you wait until tonight. I promise you a performance you'll never forget."

"I'm looking forward to watching you both perform," Aurora said diplomatically. "It's a joy to have you both here."

"I'm happy to be here," Fanny said, "even if it means I have to go on before someone as old, talentless, and mean as Bathsheba."

I choked on my laugh and turned away before strolling to the stone circle with Wiggles.

"It looks like we're in for an entertaining evening," he said. "Those two will be at each other's throats before the night is out."

"I don't doubt it." I rested a hand on a stone, and it thrummed with a heady mix of ancient magic. "Bathsheba does seem up herself. We'd better keep an eye on her to make sure she doesn't spoil Granny Dottie's birthday surprise."

Aurora hurried over and grabbed my elbow. "It's going well, don't you think?"

"Sure. We just need to keep those two spitfires out of each other's way and it should be okay." I glanced back to see the two singing divas giving each other the stink eye. "This had better be worth it."

Aurora grinned. "Oh, it will be. Granny Dottie will love her surprise. I can't see anything going wrong."

I loved Aurora's optimism. But tonight had difficult written all over it.

Chapter 3

I left Aurora in charge of Bathsheba and Fanny and headed back to Cloven Hoof. I wanted to check that everything was running smoothly before we opened this evening.

I walked into the quiet calm of the club. You'd have never known there'd been a wild party here the night before involving a lot of sparkly magic and sticky drinks. My bar crew were awesome at their jobs.

Merrie was behind the bar, restocking the shelves. She turned and smiled. "How's everything going at the stone circle?"

"We're almost ready," I said. Somehow, we'd managed to keep the birthday surprise between Aurora and me. But at three o'clock this afternoon, we'd sent a message to everyone via the snow globe network to tell them to be at the stone circle at nine thirty that evening.

The only one who hadn't gotten that message was Granny Dottie, and she was currently elbow deep in patrolling the demon prison and would hopefully be none the wiser about tonight's surprise.

"I can't believe you arranged this," Merrie said. "It's going to be incredible."

"You have my sister to thank for that. When she's determined to get something, she digs in her heels and goes for it. She left ten messages before she got a reply from Bathsheba's assistant."

"I'm glad she's done it," Merrie said. "I love Bathsheba Delaware. I have several live recordings of her early concerts. She has such a natural talent."

"She's also naturally talented at being difficult," I said. "So long as she sings well tonight and makes Granny Dottie happy, that's all I'm worried about."

"I can't wait."

"Are you bringing anyone with you tonight?" I waggled my eyebrows.

Merrie grinned. "Do you mean, am I bringing Axel as my date?"

"You did look cozy last night. Are things getting serious?" I leaned against the bar.

"We've been together a while now," Merrie said. "It's moving in the right direction."

"Which would be where? Marriage? Getting a house together and having lots of half-demon babies running around?"

Merrie grimaced. "That is a small problem. Axel's rather terrifying father. If things really did get serious between us, I'd have to meet Kroni. I'm not sure that's a safe thing to do."

"It definitely wouldn't be safe," I said. "I suggest you dodge that bullet. I've met Kroni. He's not an easy demon to handle. He tends to slaughter first and ask questions later."

"Axel doesn't talk about him much," Merrie said. "But I know they're in touch. I'll just have to deal with it when the time comes."

"Let me know if you need any help with that. I've got a few years of experience handling troublesome demons."

Merrie chuckled. "Of course. How is Frank behaving? I've not noticed him around much."

"Our relationship is currently on the far end of the complicated scale. He's giving me the silent treatment. And I'm getting used to it. It's nice not to have him inside my head, whispering all his murderous thoughts to me. Although when he doesn't come out to play for a few months, it makes my skin itch."

"Better that he's quiet rather than causing chaos every five minutes." Merrie stacked another row of drinks on the shelf.

"You've got that right." I pushed away from the bar. "I've got some paperwork to finish in the back office."

Merrie nodded. "No worries. I'll keep an eye on things out here. I'm not expecting a big rush tonight."

I nodded thanks and headed into the office with a lemon drop and a bowl of dried mushrooms cultivated by the warlocks of Peru.

Wiggles settled in the corner of the office and went straight to sleep, while I got my head down and dug through a pile of boring but necessary admin.

The next time I checked the clock, it was almost nine o'clock in the evening.

I hopped up, nudged Wiggles awake, and we headed out through the now open bar.

Merrie was just leaving, Axel by her side. She waved at me as she headed out the door. "Paula's got the bar covered. We'll see you at the stones."

I raised a hand in acknowledgement and nodded.

Paula and Izzie were in charge of the club tonight. I expected it to be a quiet evening after the craziness of yesterday. Most people would be at the stone circle waiting to enjoy a free concert or having an early night after over-indulging.

"Bring us back a recording," Izzie shouted.

"Will do," I said. I shrugged on my jacket as we walked out into the cool night air and strode over to the cemetery. It was my job to collect Granny Dottie and take her to her surprise.

We headed to the large black ornate gates and into what, on the surface, appeared to be a normal cemetery. You didn't have to dig for long to realize this was the largest demon prison in the world. It housed some of the biggest, baddest, and most evil demons ever known. And my family had guarded them for centuries.

"Knock knock." I poked my head around an open crypt door.

Granny Dottie jerked upright in the seat she was slumped in and swiped a hand across her mouth. "What? I wasn't sleeping. I simply had my eyes shut for a moment. I was deep in thought." She blinked rapidly at me.

"Sure you were. Come on. Your shift's over." I strolled into the crypt. "I'm guessing the demons behaved themselves tonight?"

"They always do when I'm on duty. They know better than to mess with me." Granny Dottie stood and placed the lid on her empty cake tin. "What are you doing here? You're not taking over the late shift."

"I'm definitely not here for guard duty."

Her eyes narrowed. "So, what are you doing here?"

I grinned. "It's another birthday surprise."

Granny Dottie's eyes glittered. "Another one? After my amazing party at your club last night. What have I done to deserve this?"

I gave her a kiss on the cheek. "You've been our awesome granny. Let's move. We don't want to be late."

"How exciting. But where's your mom? She's got the next shift."

"It's all in hand. We'll see Mom soon." It was unusual to leave the demon prison unattended, but we could do it for a short amount of time if we put the right spells in place. I didn't want any of the family missing out on the celebrations this evening.

"Will there be other people at this surprise?" Granny Dottie asked.

"A lot of them," I said.

"I should go home and change. Is this a glamorous event?"

"You look beautiful just as you are." I brushed cake crumbs off the front of her shirt. "And we need to hurry. We can't miss the start."

Her mouth formed a surprised O. "Can you give me a tiny hint?"

"It's in the village, and it's one of your favorite things."

"Is it Tate, laid out on a table naked, with one of his delicious pizzas resting on his washboard stomach?"

I choked out a laugh. "How do you know Tate has a washboard stomach?"

"I like to imagine he has. It always puts a smile on my face when I think of him naked."

"No one's getting naked tonight," I said. "It's not that sort of party."

"You never know. Your grandad still has some energy left in him."

I poked my fingers in my ears. "La la la la. Not listening."

She yanked one of my hands down. "It's good to have a healthy love life, no matter what your age. And I've seen a glow on your cheeks ever since you got serious with Rhett."

"Let's move on from this hideously uncomfortable conversation." I grabbed her elbow and propelled her out of the crypt. "We have somewhere we need to be. Are you ready?"

"We're not walking?"

"If we walk, you can guarantee someone will give the game away. Put this on." I pulled a black blindfold from out of my jacket pocket.

"What is this, some kind of saucy bondage club we're going to?"

"Is that where you really want to go?" I helped to adjust the blindfold over her eyes.

"It's important to experience life. You don't know what you like until you try everything."

"Whatever you say, Granny." I shook my head and caught hold of her hand. "Are you ready?"

"Absolutely. Take me to my surprise," she said.

I did a quick check-in with the demon prison. The demons were quiet, and the spells were holding them in place. We'd be good to leave them on their own for several hours without the risk of an escape attempt.

I scooped Wiggles up under one arm and performed a translocation spell. We appeared at the edge of the stone circle.

I placed Wiggles on the ground and looked around. The air hummed with excitement, and the chairs lined up in front of the temporary stage were full of villagers, from Petra Duke to Puddles Lavern. It looked like nobody wanted to miss out on this performance.

"Can I look yet?" Granny Dottie whispered. "Where are we? I can hear voices."

"You can take the blindfold off now," I said.

Granny Dottie yanked it down her face and stared at all the people. "What are we doing here?"

Aurora raced over and hugged her. "You're right on time. We're five minutes away from the warmup act."

"Warmup act?" Granny Dottie looked around. "Is there a performance going on tonight?"

"Bathsheba Delaware is here to sing for you." Aurora squeaked and bounced on her toes.

Granny Dottie's mouth fell open. "Here? In Willow Tree Falls? She's singing for me?"

"She is!" Aurora hugged her again. "Happy birthday, Granny."

She placed a hand over her heart, and a huge smile lit her face. "What have I done to deserve such wonderful granddaughters? She's my favorite singer."

"We know," I said. "That's all you used to listen to when we were growing up. Every morning, you'd try to sing along to Bathsheba in the shower."

"Isn't she wonderful?" Granny Dottie said. "A real talent."

"And she's here tonight. You're the special guest of honor," Aurora said. "We've saved you a seat in the front row next to Grandpa."

"Wait! I can't go to the concert without a bit of glam." Granny Dottie stepped back and ran her hands over her hair and down her body. Her hair was transformed into a glittering powderpuff of curls as a shimmering gown slid over her. She turned her attention to me and frowned.

I held up my hands and backed away. "I don't need to change. I'm fine as I am."

Her lips pursed. "You're wearing all black."

"It's my favorite color."

She jabbed a finger out, and magic shot toward me. "It's my birthday surprise. I get to choose the outfits."

I groaned as I looked down at the skin-tight white jeans and floaty red top I now wore. "Really?"

She chuckled and kissed my cheek. "You look beautiful."

"What about Aurora?" I scowled at my sister, who was decked out in a fitted sixties style red swing dress.

"She always looks presentable." Granny Dottie grabbed Aurora's hand. "Take me to my seat."

Aurora led her over to the row of seats at the front. After saying hello to as many people as possible, Granny Dottie finally settled in the center seat in the front aisle next to Grandpa Lucius, her hands clasped in her lap and wonder on her face.

We'd only been settled for a few moments when the lights around the temporary stage dimmed.

I glanced over my shoulder and saw a sound engineer deck where Picasso sat, his intense gaze on the controls.

Light flooded across the audience, and when my eyes adjusted, Fanny stood resplendent in a floor-length black gown, her raven hair piled on top of her head, and her eyes framed in dramatic green and gold make-up.

Her gaze traveled slowly over the crowd, who were silent as they watched her, tension creeping up as they waited for her to begin.

As Fanny took a big intake of air, the crowd seemed to copy her. Then the night sprang to life with a sweet melody as Fanny began to sing. Her song rose in tempo, and the stone circle that sat right behind the stage framed her perfectly. It sparked and shimmered with magic in rolling pulses, matching the cadence of her song. We weren't the only ones enjoying Fanny's stunning music.

The crowd oohed and aahed as the stone circle flashed lights and magic in time with Fanny's singing.

"You're such clever girls," Granny Dottie whispered. "Even our stone circle is celebrating my birthday."

It was quite a sight. I'd never seen the stones behave like this. They had their moments of erratic behavior, especially when there were bad vibes around. I guess the stone circle was a music fan.

Fanny sang six amazing songs, and when she finished, she was met with a rapturous applause and calls for an encore when she bowed to the crowd.

The lights dimmed, and she disappeared off the stage. The shimmers of magic from the stone circle also ended.

The stage light slowly grew again, and Charlotte stepped onto the stage, dressed in a sleek black cocktail dress. "Welcome everyone to an evening of music with Bathsheba Delaware. We're delighted to be here tonight to celebrate a very special lady's birthday. Let's all take a moment to give Dottie Crypt a big round of applause and wish her a very happy birthday."

The crowd happily obliged, cheering and whooping as Granny Dottie stood and waved at everyone, grinning broadly before she sat back down.

"Now it's time for the main event. Ladies and gentlemen, please welcome to the stage the renowned international opera singer and friend to the stars, Bathsheba Delaware."

Charlotte hurried off, and after a couple of minutes of waiting, Bathsheba stepped onto the stage. She was covered in a shimmering gold fabric that started at her neck and ended at the tips of her toes. Her arms were bare other than a tangle of gold bangles on her wrists. Her fingers were covered in glittering rings.

She stopped, and her gaze ran over the crowd but not in the friendly way Fanny's had done. From her haughty gaze and wrinkled nose, she appeared to be displeased with what she saw.

"My apologies for the poor performance from my warmup act," she said. "It's hard to get truly great opera singers these days. It's a dying art. I'm glad to see that you all stayed to hear a real opera singer perform."

"That's not necessary," I muttered. "Fanny was great, and I don't even like opera."

"She was excellent," Granny Dottie said. "There's no need to be rude about her."

"Maybe she was too good," Aurora said. "I don't think I've heard Bathsheba sing like that for a long time."

"She should stop running down the other singer and get on with it," Granny Dottie said. "Prove that she's the better singer of the two if she has an issue with Fanny."

"She might be a better singer, but that doesn't make her a better person," I muttered.

Bathsheba turned her back on the crowd and spread her arms wide over her head. She stayed in that position for thirty seconds as a deep crescendo of string instruments built around her.

When she turned back to the waiting audience, there was a fire in her eyes as she blasted us with the first note of her song.

My limbs softened, and I sank back in my seat. Her voice was spectacular. Every note washed over me like a warm, welcome wave. My eyes felt heavy, but I didn't dare shut them in case I missed something. Bathsheba was exquisite.

After watching her slacked jaw for several musical numbers, I forced my gaze away from the stage, and my stomach hitched. Everyone looked the same as I felt. They'd been dumbstruck by Bathsheba's voice.

I shook my head, feeling dizzy. Something felt wrong. Bathsheba's singing was too pure. Nobody hit every note perfectly, but she was doing just that and seemingly without any effort.

I focused hard on her and detected a faint shimmer coming from her skin. That wasn't her real singing voice. She was using magic to make herself sound this incredible.

Fanny hadn't done that. Her voice had been raw and emotional, and sometimes a little off key, but she'd meant every note she'd sung.

I glanced at Granny Dottie. She was enraptured by the singing. I didn't want to burst her bubble by pointing out what Bathsheba was doing. It wasn't harming anybody, even if it was deceitful.

Now I'd seen through her magical facade, I was no longer impressed. I much preferred Fanny's singing. I'd be sure to tell her so at the end of the concert.

The stone circle also appeared to have cottoned onto the fact Bathsheba wasn't being truthful with her audience. After a first few splats of magic, it had died down and was silent as she continued to sing.

Almost an hour passed before Bathsheba ended her performance. She gave a curt nod to the crowd, not even bothering to acknowledge why she was there, and strode off the stage.

There was rapturous applause when she left, and everyone started talking, commenting on how amazing the concert had been.

Granny Dottie turned to me and wiped a finger against the corner of her eye. "That was such a wonderful gift. I should scold you both for being so extravagant."

"You're more than worth it," Aurora said.

"That was really wonderful, girls." Mom stood from her seat. "How about we head back home and I make everyone some hot chocolate?"

"I'd love to, but I need to go home and check on Bandit," Aurora said.

"I noticed she wasn't here," I said. "She's still not feeling well?"

"She refused to budge from her bed," Aurora said. "I had to leave her behind in the store. I'm a bit worried about her."

"Well, let's get you home," Mom said to Granny Dottie. "This has been quite an adventure."

"Yes! Such a wonderful evening," Granny Dottie said. "I'll remember this day for the rest of my life." After kissing Aurora and me on the cheeks, she headed off with Mom and the rest of the family as the crowd dispersed.

Aurora grabbed my hand. "Is there any chance you can look in on Bathsheba and Fanny and see if they need anything? I really do need to get back to Bandit."

I grimaced. "Fine. You go. I'll deal with Mrs. I-Used-Magic-To-Sound-Amazing."

Aurora jerked her head back. "She did what?"

"No one else noticed, but Bathsheba used a spell to make us think she had a perfect singing voice."

"Oh! That's poor form." Aurora stared at the stage. "She sounded great."

"Too great. She tricked us."

Her mouth twisted to the side. "Let's not mention this to Granny. She'll only be disappointed that one of her idols isn't as amazing as she thought she was."

"Fine by me. But if Bathsheba gives me any trouble, I'm not biting my tongue."

"Please be nice," Aurora said.

"How's this for a deal; I'll be as nice to her as she is to me."

Aurora bit her bottom lip. "Maybe I should stay."

"No! I'll be on my best behavior. I'll check that everything's okay and leave them to it. I'm sure they don't want to be bothered by us after putting on a performance like that."

"Thanks. It'll take you a couple of minutes. I'm sure they won't want for anything." Aurora hurried off.

I headed toward the large red tent, just as an explosion of sparks shot out the top of the stone circle and showered around me.

I dodged several of them and brushed one off my sleeve. It was hot and would have burned if it had hit skin.

"What's up with the stone circle?" Wiggles asked.

"Maybe it's asking for an encore." A white blast shot from the stones, almost taking my head off.

"Jeez! Let's hustle before the circle goes into overdrive and turns us into ash." I dashed toward the tent.

I froze as a scream rang through the night air. It was followed by a blinding flash of light from inside the tent and several more yells and screams.

"Did the stone circle do something to the singers?" Wiggles cocked his head, his ears up.

I dashed to the entrance, my heart pounding. I pulled open the flap and discovered it was pitch black inside. Not the normal black of night. There was no light inside as if it had been sucked out.

Whatever this was, it wasn't natural.

I edged into the tent, Wiggles glued to my ankle, and cast a ball of light over my head.

I sucked in a breath. Bathsheba sat in a large gold chair, her head back and her eyes wide. There was a smoking hole in her chest.

Chapter 4

The smell of burning skin filled my nose as I took another step into the tent, my heart thundering and my mouth dry.

Liam look like he'd been frozen to the spot next to his dead wife, but then he suddenly blinked, and his gaze whipped to me.

I shook off my shock and raced over to Bathsheba. "What happened?"

"I... I have no idea." Liam sucked in a deep breath. "One second we were talking, and then everything went black. Someone came into the hospitality suite."

"Someone? Who?" I leaned over Bathsheba. There was no coming back from this injury. The shot had gone in the front and straight out the back of her. "Wiggles, check the tent. Make sure there's no one lurking in the shadows."

"On it." He bounded away.

Liam's gaze went to Bathsheba. He staggered to the side. "Is she..."

I glanced at the hole in her chest, my stomach turning over. "She's gone."

He gulped loudly, swayed from side to side, and fainted.

I sighed. Just what we needed. A man with a weak stomach. I stepped over Liam and double-checked that Bathsheba was definitely dead. There was no pulse. Magic wasn't bringing her back from this.

A sob had my head whipping around, and I winced. Charlotte and Picasso sat in the gloom by the entrance to the tent on a green and gold chaise lounge. Their faces were pale and their eyes wide as they stared at their dead mother.

I turned, blocking their view. "Did you see what happened?"

Charlotte shook her head. "I'm not sure. It was two men. They came in through the back entrance. They demanded Mom give them her jewels. She resisted, and they got angry. Then everything went dark."

My gaze flicked to Picasso. His skin was tinged with gray, and he was clutching his left arm. "Have you been injured?"

He gave a small nod. "I shouted for the men to stop and they attacked me."

Wiggles returned from his investigation of the tent. "No one else is in here, but there are two people outside running away."

"That must be the guys who robbed Bathsheba," I said. "Charlotte, keep an eye on your brother; check his injury. Do you know any healing magic?"

"A little," she whispered.

"Use it." I raced out the back entrance of the tent with Wiggles and spotted two figures in the distance racing ahead of us.

"Let's get them." Magic sparked on my fingertips as anger heated my veins. Commit a crime in Willow Tree Falls, and you had to pay.

"With pleasure." Wiggles raced ahead, smoke billowing from his nose.

I ran behind him, closing the distance until I was within firing range of the two men. I conjured a lightning bolt. "Stop right there!"

One of the guys glanced over his shoulder. His eyes widened, but he kept running.

"Don't say I didn't warn you." I flung the lightning bolt.

It smashed between them, and they stumbled but carried on running.

Wiggles was closing the gap on them too. He coughed out a fireball that narrowly missed the guy on the left.

I gathered up a pile of fist-sized rocks from the ground and spun them toward the men in a whirlwind spell. They smashed against them, and several rocks bounced off their backs, making them stumble again.

One of the men fell to the ground. Wiggles was on him a few seconds later.

"Hold him," I said. "I'll get the other one."

The remaining man was gasping for breath and his pace was slowing, but he was getting near the trees. Once he was in the forest, it would be easier to conceal himself.

I slowed, aimed a fire bolt, and let it fly. This time, it wasn't a warning shot I let loose.

It slammed into his back, and he yelped as he hit the ground face-first.

I reach him a few seconds later and rolled him onto his front to extinguish the fire blazing on his jacket.

I dropped down and pressed my knee against his chest, hovering another fire bolt over his head. "Why did you kill Bathsheba?"

He was dark-haired, scruffy, and had several days of stubble on his chin.

His head jerked back as he gasped in ragged breaths. "I don't know what you're talking about."

"You were seen running from the scene of the crime. Was it you or your friend who killed her?"

"Lady, you're not making any sense. We didn't kill anybody."

"What were you doing here? Out for an evening stroll?" I didn't recognize him. He didn't live in the village.

"We were just... I mean, we're not killers." His panicked gaze shot from side to side. "We were after the jewels."

"You killed Bathsheba for her jewelry?"

"No! Here, take them back." He pointed to the bag that lay beside him. "That's what we came here for. Nobody got killed."

I grabbed the bag and pulled it open. Inside was a pile of glittering gemstones, pearls, and bangles. I tossed the bag to the ground. "You killed Bathsheba and injured her son for these?" I growled in his face.

"You've got it all wrong. That wasn't me."

"Then it was your buddy." I grabbed the front of his shirt and hauled him to his feet. I pulled him back to where Wiggles was guarding the other guy on the ground.

"Wiggles, go get the angels. They need to be involved in this."

Wiggles jumped to his feet and bounded off.

I ducked as a huge spark of magic shot from the stone circle.

"What's with that thing?" The guy on the ground stared at the stones. He was thin, blond, with a long nose and narrow eyes.

"The stone circle is angry with you," I said. "You've just committed murder right next to it. It doesn't approve of dark magic. It messes with the positive vibes."

"Murder!" His gaze went to the man I had hold of. "What's she talking about?"

"Are they the killers?" Charlotte hurried toward me with Picasso leaning against her. "These men killed Mom?"

"It looks like it," I said. "I found her jewels on them."

"That's what they were after," Picasso said. "When they charged in, they demanded all of her jewels. She tried to fight them, and... and they killed her."

The men stared at each other in silence.

"You shouldn't be here," I said to Charlotte and Picasso. "The angels are on their way. They'll deal with these two."

Charlotte wiped her eyes and nodded. Her tear-filled gaze went to the men. "Why did you do it?"

"This is a big mistake," the guy I had hold of said.

"You're right there," I said. "You've both made a huge mistake. You're going to pay for it." I glanced at Charlotte. "Get Picasso out of here. Make sure his injury is properly looked at. We have a hospital in the village if he needs to go there."

Picasso shook his head. "The wound's not deep. Healing spells should fix it."

"Then go do that," I said. "I'll keep an eye on these two and make sure they don't get away."

Charlotte glared at both men before turning and leading Picasso back to the tent.

I shook the guy I held. "Let's start with your names. Who are you?"

The man I had hold of gulped. "I'm Mack Vale. And I'm not a killer."

"Sure you aren't, Mack." I poked the toe of my boot into the other man's side. "And you?"

"Coleman Archer. I'm also not a killer."

"One of you did it," I said. "There's a woman back there with a smoking hole in her chest and a load of missing jewels. That's not connected?"

Mack rubbed the back of his neck. "I mean, we took the jewels. She was dripping in them. She could afford to donate a few to a good cause."

"And you thought she'd be easy to steal from? What did she do, fight back, and you didn't like it?"

"She sure had a mouth on her," Coleman said gruffly. "She told us we were peasants and to leave."

"I bet that made you angry," I said.

"It didn't exactly make me happy," Coleman said with a grunt.

"But we still didn't kill her," Mack said. "At least, I didn't."

"Hey! Hang on a second. Neither did I," Coleman said. "Don't pin this on me. We were both there, but only for one thing. We didn't want to kill the old girl."

"And yet she's dead," I said.

"Incoming!"

I flicked my head back at the sound of Wiggles' voice overhead.

Three angels descended from the sky, Dazielle, Dominic, and Jophiel, who held Wiggles out at arm's length, her pretty face a mask of disgust.

Coleman rolled to his feet and made a dash for it.

As the angels landed, Wiggles leaped out of Jophiel's hands and raced after Coleman, shooting fire out of his mouth until Coleman dropped to the ground and rolled into a ball to protect himself from the flames.

The angels charged after Coleman and surrounded him as Wiggles trotted back to me, looking smug. "Job done. You see, I do have my uses."

I petted his head. "Of course, you do. Good work."

Dazielle strode over a moment later. "Wiggles believes there's been a murder."

"Wiggles believes right," I said. "You'll find what's left of Bathsheba Delaware in that big red tent over there. These guys shot her when she decided not to go down without a fight. They've also hurt her son. He's with his sister getting treatment for an arm injury."

Dazielle blinked. "That's quite an evening of entertainment you laid on. It's a shame I missed it."

"Your invitation must have gotten lost in the post," I said.

"I got my invitation." Dominic strode over, a cheery smile on his face. "I couldn't make it because I was on duty."

Dazielle glared at him. "Not that it matters. We wouldn't have come, anyway."

"Sure, you wouldn't," I said.

"Why did they kill Bathsheba?" Dazielle asked.

"I caught this one, Mack, with a bag full of Bathsheba's jewels. It was a robbery gone wrong."

"Nah! You got it all messed up, lady. It was just a robbery," Mack said. "We slipped into the back of the tent, grabbed as many jewels as we could, and headed out."

"After killing Bathsheba," I said.

Mack groaned. "That wasn't me."

"You're both implicated," Dazielle said. "One of you will go down for murder and one as an accomplice. Whoever talks first gets the better deal. It's up to you. Do you want to serve a long spell inside for your friend back there?"

Mack's mouth flapped open and closed several times. "I... I... it wasn't me."

"It was your accomplice?" Dazielle asked.

He scrubbed his chin. "I mean, it may have been. I don't wanna go to prison for this."

"You're going to prison for something," I said. "Robbery will get you less time than murder, but I'm no expert."

"Correct," Dazielle said. "Which is why we'll take it from here."

I took a step back and held up my hands. "With pleasure. This case is all yours." I turned to walk away.

"Oh, Tempest, before you go," Dazielle said. "Do you know anything about this?"

I turned, and my gut clenched. Dazielle held aloft a crimson feather. "Um, will you believe me if I say no?"

Her pale blue gaze turned steely.

I failed not to panic. I was in so much trouble. My illicit dealings with Isaac Dubrov and his noisy parrot had just been uncovered.

Chapter 5

Dazielle tucked the crimson feather inside her pocket, a sour expression on her face. "We'll discuss this another time. For now, I'll tell you that I'm aware of your involvement with a recent break-in at Angel Force."

I widened my eyes in an attempt to look innocent. "You must have me mixed up with someone else. I get that a lot." Did she know that I'd given Isaac the station's layout in exchange for information about my dad's whereabouts?

She arched an eyebrow. "You're not getting away with it. But first, I have to deal with these two. You're on my to-do list, though. Very close to the top."

"What are you planning on doing when you get around to me?"

"Make you regret talking to the wrong people."

I grimaced. I'd crossed the line by sharing that information, but Isaac had said he'd be discreet. There'd been no mention of leaving a huge feather behind. I could wring that bird's neck. But this was my mess. I'd deal with it.

The stone circle shot out a shower of hot sparks that danced around us.

Dazielle brushed several off her wings. "Why are the stones so unhappy?"

"Murder makes them grumpy," I said. "Although I've never seen them behave quite like this. They were having a great time when Fanny performed."

"Blood spilled around something so powerful will leave a mark," Dazielle said.

"Those stones won't hurt us, will they?" Mack said, one beady eye fixed on the fading light of the magic sparks coming out of the circle.

"Fortunately for you, you killed the stone circle's least favorite singer of the night. You should be okay," I said. "Although I wouldn't recommend hanging around here for long. Dazielle will find you a nice comfy cell while she decides what to do with you."

His jaw wobbled, and panic filled his gaze. "I'll put my hands up to the robbery. But I didn't kill that rude lady with the red hair."

I stared hard at Mack and pursed my lips. Coleman and Mack had been shocked when they'd learned that Bathsheba was dead. And they really didn't seem like killers. They were clumsy, weak magic users. They'd barely fought back when I'd chased after them with Wiggles. They were all fists and attitude, not killer blasts of magic.

"Have you got anyone back at Angel Force to run these two through your system?" I asked Dazielle.

"Of course. I'll do that when we take them back," she said. "I've no doubt they'll have long rap sheets."

"We're not that bad! We've only been caught a few times," Coleman said. "But we're not going down for murder. You won't find any mention of that on our records."

"You were caught red-handed," Dazielle said. "This is an open and shut case."

"Use the spell that killed Bathsheba," I said to them.

"Tempest! That's enough from you. We have everything we need to resolve this matter," Dazielle said.

"I'm curious," I said. "A magic bolt spell takes some doing. In case you hadn't noticed, neither of these two are sparking with the strong stuff. If we weren't tuned into the magic energy, they could pass as everyday folk."

"It doesn't mean they didn't do it," she said.

"It does! We can't produce a spell of that power," Mack said. "I'm a low-level warlock. I've struggled with my magic since I was a kid. I'm good for nothing. That's what my dad used to tell me. I decided to live up to his low expectations. I don't take from people who can't afford it, but a man's got to live."

"You're a regular Robin Hood," Dazielle said.

"Do the magic bolt spell," I said. "Let's see what you've got."

Dazielle sighed. "If they do the spell, will that keep you quiet and out of my business?"

"If they prove to me they've got the power to create a magic bolt that kills a person, I won't speak to you for the rest of the year."

"That's a deal I'll readily accept," Dazielle said. "No interference from a Crypt witch is on my vision board."

I arched an eyebrow. "And how's that working out for you?"

"So far, not so good." She glanced at Mack. "Go ahead. Conjure the spell."

Mack shook his head. "It won't work. I already said I'm not that kind of warlock."

"Give it your best shot," I said. "Show us the most powerful spell you can produce. Don't aim it at any of us. Direct it toward the stones. They'll absorb any excess magic you fire at them."

Mack shrugged. "This is a waste of time." He lifted his hands and closed his eyes. Magic sparked on the ends of his fingers. It slid out in a slow wave before dropping a few feet away and fizzling into nothing.

"That's it?" I peered at the dying magic.

He glanced at me. "Yup. That's the best I've got to offer. Told you, I'm good for nothing. I can't even get a simple robbery right."

"Was that really your best effort?" I asked.

"I don't have the skill. My dad blames some distant relative for marrying someone without magic. It diluted the ability. I don't know about that, though. We're not a family known for our magic skills."

"How about you?" I lifted my chin and looked at Coleman. "Let's see what you can do."

Jophiel, who was holding onto Coleman to prevent another escape attempt, released him and stepped back.

Coleman rolled his shoulders. "I'm not much better. I can do more damage than him, though."

"Enough damage to kill Bathsheba?" Dazielle asked.

"Nah! Nothing like that," he said.

"Did you create the darkness spell inside the tent?" I asked. "When I stepped inside, all the light had been sucked from the room."

"That wasn't us," Coleman said. "We didn't use any magic in that tent."

"How did you expect to beat several magic users without using your own powers?" Dazielle asked.

"Brains stop working properly under stress. Sometimes, people are so surprised at being robbed that they hand over everything," Mack said.

"Yeah, if you're mean enough and sound like you'll turn nasty, they usually cooperate," Coleman said.

"This one had a knife on him." Jophiel jabbed a finger at Coleman.

He lifted a hand. "Just for show. It's another intimidation trick I like to use. Wave a blade about and it gets people nervous. We grabbed the jewels and left. We weren't that far away when we heard the yelling but didn't wait around to see what was going on."

"That's when you came after us." Mack nodded at me. "We had no choice but to make a run for it."

"Try the magic bolt spell," I said to Coleman.

"This is a waste of time." He turned toward the stone circle, thrust his hands out, and a shiver of gray magic twisted in the air, curling up and spiraling before dissipating.

There was no way that was powerful enough to kill someone. At the worst, it might make you itch if it made contact.

Dazielle was looking on, her tart expression suggesting how unimpressed she was.

I leaned closer to her. "Those weren't killer spells."

She snorted. "They're faking it. They're more powerful than they're letting on. It's possible for a magic user to mask their true strength. It won't be the first time I've come up against someone who attempted such a deception."

"This seems different. To kill someone, you need that spark of darkness inside you."

"There's plenty of darkness among these two," Dazielle said. "I just need to get them to confess. One of them will break before long."

I wasn't so sure about that. I strode over to Mack, who cringed away from me. "Give me your hand."

"Why? What are you going to do to it?"

"See if you're lying." I grabbed his hand and held on tight. There was nothing there. When a person used magic for a negative purpose, it left a sort of stain, and I could sense that they'd slid to the dark side. I might not always know what they'd done, but I could usually tell if someone used dark magic on a regular basis.

Although there was plenty of murkiness lingering around Mack, he was no killer.

I did the same to Coleman and got exactly the same result. He was a shady character, someone who was used to lying every day, but he wasn't a murderer.

Either they were great at hiding the truth, or we had the wrong people. But if they didn't kill Bathsheba, then who did?

Dazielle cleared her throat. "When you've finished messing around with my prisoners, may I take them to Angel Force to obtain their statements and put them behind bars for murder?"

"You will question them properly?" I asked.

"When do I ever not do a proper investigation?"

I opened my mouth to cite numerous examples but then thought better of it. She was already in a bad mood with me. "I'm not getting a murder vibe from them."

"Tempest, they're deceiving you. I didn't realize you were so easy to fool," Dazielle said.

I glowered at her. "It's not that. Test their magic for yourself. You'll see that they're not capable of producing that killer magic bolt. That hole through Bathsheba's chest was caused by one heck of a powerful spell. Neither of these guys have enough power to create that."

"Most likely because they drained their power using it to kill Bathsheba," Dazielle said. "Now, do I need to repeat myself? Hands off. This is our case."

"Hey! I'm being helpful. I was the one who brought Bathsheba to Willow Tree Falls," I said. "But for her family's sake, I'd like to make sure you've got the right people in custody for her murder."

"As do we. We'll do a complete investigation, but I won't be reporting back to you about our findings," Dazielle said.

"I could always sit in on the interviews."

Dazielle's wings extended. "Stay away from Angel Force. Let me deal with this investigation. Then we'll discuss the crimson feather found in our evidence room and where the missing evidence is. I shall look forward to your explanation about that."

My mouth twisted to the side, and a shiver of unease ran through me. I had some serious explaining to do. It was clear from Dazielle's sharpness that she no longer trusted me. Maybe she never had.

"You said that someone else was injured during the attack." Dazielle said. "Where is he?"

"Picasso Delaware. He went off with his sister, Charlotte," I said. "He was hit in the arm. It didn't look too bad. He was able to walk just fine."

"Jophiel, go see to Bathsheba's children. We need to get their statements as soon as possible. Make sure the son receives any treatment he needs," Dazielle said.

"There's also the husband, Liam," I said. "The last time I saw him, he'd passed out next to the body. They were all there when Mack and Coleman broke in."

"Yes, thank you, Tempest. We have this in hand. You don't need to stay any longer. Don't you have a club to run?"

I shrugged and turned, gesturing for Wiggles to follow me. I could sense when Dazielle was at the end of her tether. It had happened about five minutes ago.

Cloven Hoof would be fine without me for the evening, and since I had spare time on my hands, it wouldn't do any harm to check in with Fanny and see if she'd heard the news.

Maybe she'd have some insight into why Bathsheba was killed tonight.

Chapter 6

There was only one hotel in Willow Tree Falls, so I tried there first to see if Fanny had booked a room.

I strolled into the reception lobby to find Tabitha Dimples sitting with a book in front of her.

She slid her glasses to the top of her head and raised her eyebrows when she saw me. "Tempest! It's late. What are you doing here?"

"Looking for one of your guests," I said. "There's been an... incident. She might know something about it."

Tabitha frowned. "Whenever you're involved, the incident often relates to murder. Don't tell me there's been another slaying in the village?"

"I'm not at liberty to say," I said. I mean, I could, but it would only be another reason to make Dazielle even angrier with me. "Can you tell me if you've got Fanny Flotella staying here?"

"Oh! Of course. Such a lovely woman. She checked in this afternoon. She asked me if I was going to the concert, and of course, I received your invitation, but opera isn't my thing. I made some excuse, so she wouldn't be offended that I wasn't going."

"Has she come back from the concert yet?"

"Yes! She returned about ten minutes ago," Tabitha said. "She wasn't in a good mood though. I smiled and asked how her evening had been and if the performance went well. She simply grunted and stomped past. It was most out of character."

That put her still at the stone circle at the time Bathsheba was killed. What could have caused her mood to sour? "Which room is she in?"

"I can't tell you that." Tabitha shook her head. "Guests don't want just anyone knocking at their door."

"I only want a friendly chat."

"We all know your version of a friendly chat. It often ends up with someone getting hurt."

"That's not true!"

Her eyes widened. "How is Frank these days? Devoured any puppies recently?"

"He doesn't do that. He likes dogs." I scowled at her. "And he's as happy as a kitten with a new ball of wool. Can you at least message Fanny and tell her I'd like to see her?"

"I could try her snow globe," Tabitha said. "But I doubt she'll want to see anyone, given the mood she was in."

"Tell her it's her biggest fan," I said. "No, just tell her it's me. Make sure she knows that I thought her performance was ten times better than Bathsheba's tonight."

"It's worth a shot. That might make her open the door to you." Tabitha headed into the back room.

I could hear her muffled voice as I waited. Fanny could have seen something useful at the stone circle. Evidence that Mack and Coleman were guilty. Or if they weren't involved, then she may have spotted the person who'd killed Bathsheba. My stomach tightened. What if Fanny was involved? They were singing rivals. It may explain her bad mood.

Tabitha walked back into the lobby. "She says you can go up. It's room six."

"Thanks." I headed up the stairs with Wiggles and knocked on the door.

Fanny opened it a few seconds later. Her hair was down around her shoulders, and she wore a black silky robe. "Tempest! I was surprised to get the message from reception that you were here."

"Do you mind if I come in?"

"Since you said such nice things about me, I don't see why not." She stepped aside and allowed me into her room. "I hope everything's okay back at the stone circle."

"Not really. It's complicated," I said.

"Complicated how?" Her smile faded. "You'd better not tell me that Bathsheba sent you here."

"Why would she have sent me to see you?"

"Because that woman is out to get me." Fanny stomped to the other side of the bed and slumped into a chair by the desk. "I wouldn't put it past her to complain to you about me. I can't do a single thing right in her eyes. Whatever I do, she's disparaging and rude. Did you hear what she said about my performance before she'd even begun to sing?"

"I did," I said. "We all thought it was out of order."

"It's so typical of Bathsheba to put down anybody who threatens her."

"Have you threatened her recently?"

Fanny sat up straight. "I don't mean a physical threat. I mean a threat to her career. She destroys anybody who might dampen her fame and success. Anyone who tries to put Bathsheba in the shade is sure to be ruined. She's tried to destroy my bright star so many times, but I always come back fighting. I know dozens of fabulous singers who've had their careers destroyed because she spreads rumors about them. It's disgusting."

"If you hate her so much, why did you agree to perform here tonight?"

She sighed. "Because Bathsheba's still one of the best in the business. Even though she's washed up and past her prime, she's still incredible. If only she was a nice person, I wouldn't mind working with her. Besides, I wanted to come to Willow Tree Falls. Your sister was so charming when I spoke to her that I couldn't refuse. A big part of me wishes I hadn't bothered."

"How long has your feud with Bathsheba been going?"

"It feels like forever," Fanny said. "It's gotten bad over the last five years. I've barely seen her during that time. But it's hard to avoid her completely. There are only a few successful singers in our particular field, and we usually get booked for the same events."

"Have things ever gotten heated between you?"

"Just about every time we meet." Fanny chuckled. "I expect it now. When she first turned on me, I was shocked, but it's how Bathsheba operates. Take tonight for example; when I went to see her after the performance, she told me I wasn't getting paid."

"She can't do that," I said.

"That's what I told her, but she'd made an arrangement with your sister so the whole payment went to her and she'd distribute it to me afterward. I should have seen it coming, but I was excited to perform. She told me I wasn't getting paid because my singing was off key, and when the audience was forced to listen to me, they were in physical pain."

"That's not true," I said. "I sat in the front row and enjoyed your singing. I'll admit I'm not a big opera fan, but your performance was captivating."

Fanny's cheeks flushed, and she smiled brightly. "Thank you. After the evening I've had, that's just what I need to hear. I sometimes wonder about giving up."

"You really shouldn't," I said. "And I could tell that your singing was natural."

She stared at me before a sly smile spread over her face. "I don't know how Bathsheba does it, but she enhances her voice. She didn't use to do it, but every time she performs now, she uses some trick or piece of magic to mesmerize her audience. She's slowly losing her ability, but she won't accept it."

"I only noticed what she was doing because I glanced around at everyone in the audience. They looked like they were in a trance."

"Yes! I've seen that too. Being offstage and not directly in front of Bathsheba means her ability isn't so strong on me. I can't always see through it and get as entranced as everyone else, but now and again, I can tell she's using something to deceive people."

"And you didn't do that," I said. "Your voice was twice as lovely, and it was completely natural. You have a real talent."

She pressed a hand to her chest. "It's kind of you to say. It makes it all worthwhile."

"How was Bathsheba behaving when you last saw her?" I asked. That was enough sweet talking. I needed to get down to business before the angels dropped by and interrupted me.

"She was being her usual haughty, smug self. Her children and Liam were in the tent when I went in and asked about my payment. That was when she broke the bad news. She laughed in my face. Bathsheba told me that performing on stage before her should be payment enough. A woman has to eat! I can't live on fresh air. She swans around dripping in her jewels and thinking the world owes her, yet she's not prepared to hold a hand out and help other people up. And, although I pity her children and that gorgeous but pointless husband of hers, they did nothing to help. They sat around staring at me mutely."

"Her pointless husband?"

"Oh! Well, yes, he's a bit useless. Liam is sex on a stick but as dull as a brick. I see why she picked him, and it wasn't for his brains."

"Perhaps her family has learned that it's better not to go up against Bathsheba," I said. "It sounds like she has a temper."

"She shouts at people because they let her get away with it," Fanny said. "She was yelling at me when I was trying to get my money out of her."

I stepped closer. "And was she breathing when you left the tent?"

Fanny blinked several times. "What do you mean? Of course, she was breathing. She was sitting on that ridiculous gold throne of hers like she was a member of royalty."

"When I saw a Bathsheba less than an hour ago, she was no longer breathing."

Fanny's hand flew to her mouth, and her eyes widened. She lowered her hand and swallowed. "She's... dead? What happened? Did her heart give out? I told her to lay off the sugared doughnuts."

"It wasn't the doughnuts. She was murdered," I said. "Did you kill Bathsheba because she refused to pay you?"

"Oh! No! Absolutely not. I was furious with her and demanded that I get paid. I told her that I wouldn't stop hassling until I got what I was owed, but I'd never kill her." A warbling sob came from her mouth.

I glanced down at Wiggles. That was an odd noise. It sounded like Fanny was about to begin a performance.

She sucked in a wobbly breath and continued to warble before breaking out into a full-on opera song.

I raised a hand. "Now's not the time to sing."

"It calms me down," Fanny sang. "I get panic attacks. Terribly bad ones. My therapist told me that I had to do the one thing I love to keep me centered. I love to sing. You must sing with me. Both of you. It'll help keep me calm."

I shook my head. "You don't want me singing."

"I'll sing," Wiggles said. "I know some great sea shanties."

Fanny continued to sing, and Wiggles joined in loudly, singing off-key about some drunken old sailor who had a boat with a hole in it and only his thumb to plug it.

"Tell me everything about your last meeting with Bathsheba," I said.

Fanny shook her head. "I feel faint. You must sing, or I shall collapse."

"My singing won't—"

"Singgggggg!" she warbled out.

"You'd better do what she says," Wiggles said. "You don't want her collapsing before you've gotten the information you're after."

I gritted my teeth. I was no singer, but if it kept Fanny from having a breakdown, I had to suck it up and get on with it.

"Tell me about your last conversation with Bathsheba," I sang, shuffling from foot to foot, my face blazing.

"She was rude. She was mean. She told me I wasn't good enough," Fanny sang.

"So, you killed her?" I warbled.

"No, I didn't. I wouldn't do that. Bathsheba's a rival, but everyone knows she was past her prime."

"Everyone or just you?" I asked.

"You must keep singing the words," Wiggles said. "Your voice isn't so terrible when you get going."

I sighed. "Everyone or just you," I sang.

"Not just me," Fanny trilled. "Bathsheba even talked about booking a slot in a club, so she wouldn't have to go on any more tours. She was also talking about getting another child, which would mean fewer trips."

"Another adoption?" I sang.

"That's right. She was too old to have a baby of her own. And there's no passion from Liam. I doubt there's been much action between the sheets since their wedding night. He's a trophy husband. She reminded him of that at every opportunity."

"Did you see anyone when you left the tent after your fight with Bathsheba?"

"No one. It was late. After the concert, I gave Bathsheba time to relax. Putting on a performance is stressful." Fanny sucked in a deep breath and blasted out her next words. "I went into the hospitality suite to get my payment. We argued, and I left. By that time, the crowd had gone. I returned to the hotel and came up to my room, not wanting to see anybody."

That was a lousy alibi. She could easily have killed Bathsheba. Fanny might have seen an opportunity to strike in the chaos following the robbery. She could have snuck in, created a darkness spell to use as cover, and fired a magic bolt at Bathsheba.

If Mack and Coleman weren't involved with this murder, I'd just found a really good alternative suspect.

"Keep singing," Fanny warbled.

I sucked in a breath and joined in with Wiggles. What a ridiculous way to end the night.

Chapter 7

With a big pile of pancakes covered in syrup and chocolate chips on my plate, I was happily settled in my kitchen, sipping coffee, while Wiggles devoured several doughnuts.

"My ears are still ringing from your dodgy singing last night," he said.

"You said I wasn't terrible. And yours wasn't exactly spot on," I said. "You kept singing about drunken sailors and what they like to do with their rude bits. That wasn't useful to the investigation. At least my shrieking was an attempt to untangle what happened and get useful information from Fanny."

"And have we made progress?" Wiggles asked. "You still think those guys we caught running away from the murder are innocent?"

"There's nothing innocent about them. They had the evidence on them. They definitely robbed Bathsheba but kill her?" I shrugged. "Maybe she talked back or tried to fight them."

"They could have had a magic item on them that blasted her."

"Something like that wouldn't be cheap, though. And they didn't strike me as high rollers."

"It's possible that they don't like women who stand up for themselves," Wiggles said. "She tried to tackle them, and they fought back."

"If that happened, Bathsheba had backup in the form of her husband and her two children. They wouldn't have sat back and watched it happen."

"They wouldn't have had much choice, given how dark it was. They wouldn't have known what was going on until we arrived."

"Mack and Coleman said someone else triggered the blackout spell."

"And we believe the two criminals because..."

I shrugged. "We don't."

"Do you think Fanny could be involved in this?" Wiggles asked.

"She's got a great reason for wanting Bathsheba dead. You could tell she was angry last night that she wasn't getting paid for her performance. And Bathsheba was openly rude about Fanny's singing in front of everyone. That must have stung. Famous people often come with big egos that need a serious amount of stroking. Plus, no one can account for Fanny's whereabouts during the time of the murder. We might have just missed her when we went into the tent. She could have been heading off in one direction and the robbers in the other. We chased after the wrong people."

Wiggles chomped down on a doughnut. "I did smell her around the tent. And it was recent. We could have missed her."

"I'm not sure this murder is as straightforward as the angels think it is."

My snow globe sprung to life, and a shower of tiny snow sparkles shot around it.

I pressed the top. "Yo!"

"Tempest, your presence is requested at Angel Force." Dazielle's tone was curt.

I suppressed a groan. "I'm really busy right now. How about we meet up in a couple of weeks?"

Her face loomed into view. "You're eating pancakes. That's hardly an emergency."

"They're really good pancakes," I said. "I made them myself. It would be a crime to waste them."

"You should come join us," Wiggles said. "I've got doughnuts if you'd prefer those. I might share if you ask really nicely."

"No to the breakfast invitation," Dazielle said. "Come to the station."

"Does this mean you want my help with Bathsheba's murder?" I asked.

"This has nothing to do with that, and I absolutely don't need your help on any of my cases."

"You must need my help for something," I said. "Otherwise, you wouldn't be calling so early."

"It's nearly noon," Dazielle said. "You're fortunate I didn't come banging on your front door at dawn. We need to talk about this crimson feather discovered in the evidence room."

I frowned, and my good mood faded. There was no getting out of this. I had to face the music when it came to the deal I'd made with Isaac. "I can be there in an hour."

"Make it thirty minutes." Dazielle ended the call.

"It looks like we're going to hang out with the angels," Wiggles said.

"Be still my beating heart," I said. "Before we do, I've got pancake batter that needs whisking up and cooking."

Wiggles chuckled as he set to work on his next doughnut.

Half an hour later, we were out of the apartment. Before I faced the less than pleasant music with Dazielle, I made a detour to Aurora's store.

The second I opened the door, something felt off. There was a large crystal glowing on the counter, and several of the bottled spells on the shelves were smoking.

I stepped inside with Wiggles and cautiously closed the door. "Aurora, you in here?"

She hurried out of the back, and my mouth dropped open. Her hair was bright green.

"I'm so glad you're here," she said. "Everything's gone badly this morning."

"Including your hair," I said. "Did something go wrong with your dye job?"

She stroked a hand down the bright color. "I'm not sure what's going on with my hair. I woke up this morning with it like this."

"Are you getting sick?" Although I had no clue what illness turned a person's hair green.

"I feel fine. After the initial shock of seeing the color, I quite like it."

"You look like a beautiful head of broccoli," Wiggles said. "I'd take a bite out of you any time."

"Of course, you would. You're such a good boy." She bent and tickled him under the chin.

"And what's with the bottled spells being agitated?" I ducked as something whizzed past my head.

"I can't figure that out either. I got woken by my bed shaking. I came downstairs wondering what was going on and thought we were having an earthquake. Then I saw the chaos down here. It's been like this all morning. I've been fire fighting to keep order down here and checking on Bandit. I was just having a quick break to see if she was awake when I heard you come in."

"How's Bandit doing?" I asked.

"That's why I'm glad you're here. She's really sick. She's not faking it."

"She's really ill?" Wiggles' ears shot up. "I figured she'd had too much to drink the other night."

"I wondered if she'd overindulged as well," Aurora said. "That's why I didn't take her complaining and grumpiness seriously. But she's off her food and really hot. I'm making sure she drinks regularly, but all she wants to do is sleep. And when she sleeps, she mutters and tosses around as if she can't get comfortable."

"You should take her to see Abigail," I said.

"Oh! I hadn't thought about that. She might have something for sick familiars."

"It's worth a shot," I said. "I've never seen Bandit refuse food she likes."

"Which makes me think she isn't just looking for sympathy," Aurora said.

I dodged a spell book as it flapped off the shelf. "While I'm here, do you want me to give you a hand to settle down the magic?" Several corks popped out of spell bottles.

"Yes, please. That crystal's been glowing for half an hour. No matter what I do to it, it doesn't respond. It's like it's been magically over-charged, but I've not done anything to it."

I walked over to the crystal and hovered my hand over it. Sparkles of magic shot out and latched onto my skin. I pulled my hand away and shook it. "That's weird."

"Everything is being weird in here today. All the books jumped off the shelf a little while ago. I've only just got them back in order, and now they're flying around." She grabbed a spell book as it wobbled past, using its pages like wings.

"Since you've been busy with your misbehaving store, you won't have heard what happened after the concert," I said.

Aurora glanced at me as she grabbed several glass vials before they bounced off the shelf. "Last night? Don't tell me you had an argument with Bathsheba."

"I didn't get the chance to," I said. "She was murdered."

Aurora's mouth fell open. "Murdered! Tell me everything." She carefully placed the vials back on the shelf and secured them under a book.

"I was heading toward Bathsheba's tent, when there were flashes of light and people started yelling. When I got inside, Bathsheba had been shot through the chest with a bolt spell. Wiggles caught two guys running away with her stolen jewels, and we chased them down."

"Oh my spells! Bathsheba was killed for her jewels? She was wearing an awful lot of sparkles on stage. Someone from the village saw her and got tempted?"

"It was no one from the village. I've never seen these two guys before. Mack and Coleman. Maybe they were following Bathsheba in the hope she'd set up and perform so they could sneak in and get their hands on her treasure. However, they got here, they robbed her and made a run for it. The problem is, I'm not so sure they did kill her."

"It wasn't a robbery gone wrong?" Aurora dodged a healing stone that flew through the air and grabbed it before it could cause any damage.

"Dazielle's convinced it was them. And on the surface, they look guilty. But I tested their magic. They don't have the power to produce a killing spell. She's convinced it was them though, and they're simply masking their abilities to appear innocent."

"Is that the only reason you're doubting that they're guilty?"

I tilted my head from side to side. "Bathsheba made everyone hate her. There are a lot of people out there who'll be doing a happy dance when they learn she was killed."

"I doubt her children or her husband will be doing a happy dance," Aurora said. "They must be devastated."

"Liam." I tapped my fingers against my chin. "I hadn't thought about him as the killer. Bathsheba treated him more like a slave than a husband.

And Fanny described him as gorgeous but useless. Should I consider him a suspect as well?"

"Wait! Go back a few steps," Aurora said. "You talked to Fanny about this? You think she could be involved in killing Bathsheba?"

"I do. Get this. Bathsheba refused to pay Fanny for her performance at the stone circle. Fanny was in a foul mood when she got back to the hotel, and she admitted that they were serious rivals. Maybe she got tired of being treated like dirt by Bathsheba and killed her."

"Tempest, you need to solve this. After all, we invited Bathsheba here. No one expected her to be killed while she was in Willow Tree Falls."

"I've tried to get involved, but Dazielle made it clear that I need to keep my nose out."

Aurora shot a spell of calm at a book hovering in the air, and it floated to the floor. "Since when has that stopped you from investigating if you're interested in a case?"

"That's true. But if I was in Dazielle's position, I'd think I'd struck gold by having the killers handed to me so easily. I wouldn't want to make extra work for myself. Why should she look beyond the obvious suspects?"

"To make sure she's right?" Aurora shook her head. "The Crypt family name will be sullied if we get caught up in this scandal."

I chuckled. "It's too late for that."

Her eyes widened. "Our family name has no scandal attached to it."

"Really? How about Auntie Queenie and her former biker gang?"

"That was ages ago. Everyone's forgotten she was involved with a gang."

"How about your disastrous engagement to a deceitful manipulator who turned you into a stone dragon and used you to decorate the outside of his house?"

Aurora's cheeks flushed red. "Anyone can make a mistake."

"Okay, then how about the fact I've got a malevolent demon lurking inside me who wants to get his claws into you?"

She huffed out a breath. "Every family has its quirks."

"Ours is the quirkiest," I said.

"None of that's important. You must keep digging. You have to get to the bottom of this."

"The guys in custody are guilty of theft. That's a point to Dazielle."

"But they're not guilty of murder?"

I shook my head. "I don't think they are. Even so, I'm sitting this one out. If Dazielle does her job properly, she'll realize that they didn't kill Bathsheba."

"And if she doesn't figure it out? You know how lazy those angels can be. They find someone who's a likely suspect and only focus on them. You've seen it happen in the past. It even happened with you."

"She's getting better," I said. "I heard that she's been on a few courses. I bet she'll solve this all on her own without my help."

"All I'm saying is—" Aurora squeaked and slapped a hand over her mouth.

"All you're saying is what?"

She jabbed a finger in the air, pointing over my shoulder.

I turned and resisted the urge to shrink away as I spotted an angry Dazielle standing outside Heaven's Door. Her cheeks were flushed, and her eyes sparkled like shards of diamonds.

"Oops! I lost track of time," I said. "I was supposed to meet Dazielle."

"I've never seen her look that angry." Aurora lowered her hand. "What have you done this time? She can't be mad at you for trying to get to the truth about this murder."

"I'm sure she's angry with me about that, but there's something else on her mind."

Aurora grabbed two books as they flew through the air. "You can blame me. Say I insisted you come and help with Bandit and my naughty store."

"Maybe I should stay and look after Bandit if she really is feeling bad," Wiggles said.

"You! Look after Bandit?" I shook my head. "You'll only aggravate her. You're not getting out of this. I need backup. We need to get out of here and face one angry angel before she smashes down the door and drags us to the station in handcuffs."

Chapter 8

Dazielle's dark mood matched the rolling mass of fat, gray clouds over our heads as she marched me in silence to Angel Force.

"It's weird weather we're having this time of year," I said.

She grunted.

"I'm not making polite conversation. They look like snow clouds." I pointed at the swirling stack overhead. "Anyone would think we're heading into winter."

Dazielle slowed and glanced upward. "Much like everything today, they don't look like normal storm clouds."

"What do you —" A scream had me spinning around. A woman raced out of Sprinkles with her hair on fire. Patti was close behind her, trying to bat the flames out with her apron.

I took a step closer to offer my help when a wing folded around me.

"No, you don't. You're not getting out of this."

I batted the mass of tickly feathers out of my face. "In case you hadn't noticed, there's a woman on fire."

"Patti's dealing with it," Dazielle said. "We need to talk."

I continued to stare at the bizarre scene as Patti threw herself on the blazing woman and extinguished the flames. After a few seconds of rolling around together, Patti hopped up and helped the woman to her feet.

"Let's move, Tempest."

I nodded, glancing over my shoulder at Patti. Had she done that to a customer, or was her store misbehaving just like Aurora's was?

Thunder rumbled overhead as we reached the front doors of Angel Force.

"Wiggles, stay in the reception area," Dazielle said.

"Do I have to? I thought we'd gotten our little problem sorted out," he said. "I promise only to steal food that's been abandoned and is looking unloved."

"Sit. Stay. Do not beg." Dazielle bared her teeth.

I grimaced and shrugged at Wiggles. "Maybe you should wait here." I'd never seen Dazielle so harassed.

When we stepped into the main office, the atmosphere felt charged. Angels dashed around seemingly without direction, and the main room was full of people looking worried or tense. Everyone was talking at once, and the stress levels were off the chart, making my insides clench and my mouth go dry.

"What's going on in here?" I asked. "Was there a full moon last night? That always brings out the crazies."

"I wish I knew. This way." Dazielle marched in front of me along a white corridor and into a small room. She ushered me in and shut the door behind her.

There were two chairs and a table in the room. I sat on one chair. Dazielle remained standing, her arms crossed over her chest and her wings fluttering around her.

"So, what do you want to talk about?" I rested my hands on my lap and tried not to look guilty.

"Let's start with Bathsheba's murder," Dazielle said. "Why are you snooping about in a closed case?"

"You've closed it already? That must be a record for you. Mack and Coleman have confessed?"

"I'm asking the questions," she said. "Explain the snooping."

"What makes you think I've been snooping?"

Her eyes narrowed. "You had a conversation with Fanny Flotella last night. You informed her of Bathsheba's murder and asked about her whereabouts. As you can imagine, my angels were less than pleased when they discovered this. You could have tipped her off that we were investigating a murder. If she was involved, she might have tried to abscond."

"Hold on. I'm confused. I thought you said the two guys caught robbing Bathsheba killed her?"

She glared at me unblinking for several long seconds. "It's theoretically possible that they combined their powers or had an artificial spell enhancement."

"Theoretically? Okay, I'm reading between the lines here, but they haven't confessed? You're holding them for the robbery, but they're not admitting that they murdered Bathsheba?"

"It's only a matter of time before one of them talks," Dazielle said. "They did this."

I jumped as something crashed outside the door. "What's going on out there? I've never seen the place so busy or full of people."

She sighed and paced across the floor. "It's been like this all day. Well, since just after midnight. My angels have been pulling double shifts to meet demand."

"What's got everyone out of whack?"

"We don't know. But we've had reports of everything from frogs raining from the sky to the old wishing well bubbling over and flooding the nearby houses."

"I thought that well had run dry years ago."

"It had, and it wasn't water bubbling out of it. Anyway, we're getting off the point."

I lifted a hand. "I don't think Mack and Coleman have it in them to kill Bathsheba. They're below par magic users. You can run as many tests on them as you like, but they won't conjure up that killer spell. You're holding the wrong people."

She glared at me and huffed out a breath. "If not them, who do you think killed Bathsheba?"

"Before I answer that, does this mean you want my help?"

She squinted at me. "I can always have you arrested."

"For helping bring down two criminals?"

"For obstructing an investigation."

I raised my hands. "I'll talk. Fanny has a great motive, and she had the opportunity to kill. Did she tell you that Bathsheba refused to pay her for last night's performance at the stone circle?"

"It was mentioned."

"According to Tabitha, Fanny was raging mad when she got back to the hotel. And she only returned about ten minutes before I got to her. That would have given her plenty of time to kill Bathsheba and escape."

"Doubtful. Did you see the heels Fanny wore last night?"

"I'm not a shoe kind of woman. What did I miss?"

"They were five-inches of pure pain. You don't run in heels like that."

"So, she took them off after she killed Bathsheba," I said. "She could have run back to the hotel barefoot."

"The soles of her feet would have been damaged if that was the case. That's a good half a mile."

"Then check her feet for any grazes," I said. "I don't think you should discount her. She could have treated her feet before you spoke to her. Thinking about it, she wasn't wearing any shoes when I saw her. That could have been because her feet were sore."

"I am discounting her," Dazielle said. "We have our men."

"You don't believe that, or you wouldn't be asking for my opinion. And speaking of men, what about Liam, the disillusioned husband?"

"What has he got to be disillusioned about? He was married to an extremely wealthy woman."

"A woman who treated him like a dumb dog. She ordered him around and was dismissive of him. How long would you put up with that before snapping?"

"It wasn't Liam. He was beside Bathsheba when she was hit."

I tipped my head back. That was a valid point. "Unless he used the cover of darkness. He could have created that blackout spell then crept around in front of Bathsheba. Everyone would have been disoriented and uncertain about what was going on. It was just the opportunity he needed. He positioned himself where he knew Bathsheba was sitting and let rip with the spell."

"Why injure his son as well?" Dazielle asked.

"His stepson," I said. "Maybe they don't have a tight bond. Or Picasso tried to intervene. If he'd thrown himself blindly at the attacker and struck Liam, Liam would have needed to get Picasso away and then reposition himself next to Bathsheba. When I came in, it seemed like nothing was out of place."

"Did Liam appear flustered when you saw him?" Dazielle asked.

"No. Sort of bemused about what was happening. That was until he fainted."

She shook her head. "It's an interesting theory, but that's not what happened. Picasso said he didn't move from his seat. He was sat next to Charlotte the whole time. When the blackout spell hit, she grabbed his hand and begged him not to move because she was scared, so he didn't. He stayed by her side to protect her."

"At least talk to Fanny some more," I said. "You can't discount her because of a pair of shoes. She's got a lot to gain now Bathsheba's dead. I bet she moves up the rank in the world of opera. Maybe that's what this was all about. She was being blocked from progressing her career and had to remove an obstacle."

"We've already spoken to Fanny but only to confirm the details of the two men who killed Bathsheba."

I sighed. Once again, Dazielle had got it into her pretty but dumb head that the problem was solved. She wasn't open to other options, even though she realized this didn't fit together.

"This investigation is over. We're too busy with the other problems in the village to make this case into something it's not," Dazielle said.

"Other than the overflowing wishing well and frogs raining from the sky, what else are you dealing with?" I asked.

"Have you been to see the magic barrier recently?"

"Not since Bathsheba came through. What's it doing?"

"It's... unhappy. It keeps shivering. We've been pumping extra magic into it, but it's not stable."

I sat forward in my seat. "The magic barrier can't go down. We'll be exposed to everyone. What's messing with the barrier?"

"Probably the same thing messing with everyone else in the village. Take a look around. We're all having problems. Seeing that woman come running out of Sprinkles on fire was one of the least bizarre things I've seen today."

"Just like Aurora's store," I said. "All her potions were acting up. And did you notice the color of her hair?"

"I did. She's not the only one who woke up to changes. Some people have lost their hair entirely. I've had three incidents filed with people claiming someone snuck in while they were sleeping and shaved their heads. Not only that, but they took the hair. It had vanished."

"A hair thief?" This day just kept getting weirder.

"There's something big going on in the village. I need my angels focused on that. What we have here is a simple murder, and the killers are in our custody. Now, I want to talk to you about a more serious matter."

I ran my tongue along my top teeth. "What could be more serious than murder?"

"Stolen evidence." Dazielle stopped pacing. "What do you know about it?"

I pressed my lips together as I contemplated my response. I could straight out lie, I could give her a variation of the truth, or I could be upfront. None of the options were good.

"Your silence is speaking volumes," Dazielle said. "Tell me about this feather." She placed the crimson feather on the table.

"It looks like it's from a tropical bird. Maybe of South American origin. I'm no expert when it comes to our feathered friends. I prefer dogs."

She shook her head. "You've been seen associating with Isaac Dubrov. Everyone knows Isaac owns that rude, opinionated parrot. Should I assume it was a coincidence that you met with him, and a few weeks later, important evidence went missing from Angel Force?"

"You absolutely should," I said. It looked like I was going down the lying route. It didn't feel great.

Dazielle leaned on the table. "Isaac's a man who can get information, but he never gives that information without expecting something in return. What did you share with him?"

"I haven't even admitted to a meeting with Isaac."

"But you're not denying that you know who he is?"

"I know him by reputation," I said slowly.

She thumped a hand on the table. "We don't have time for games. Isaac is a bad person. He's dangerous to be around, and he manipulates people to get what he wants. If you gave him information about us, I have a right to throw you in a cell."

"For gossiping?"

"For being an accomplice to a break-in. For potentially undoing years of research focused on bringing down Isaac Dubrov and his corrupt crew of magic users."

"Oh! Is that what you've been doing?" Okay, I'll admit this made me feel a bit guilty. "I had no idea."

"Isaac's as slippery as an eel. We think we've got a lead on him, and then he vanishes. This time, we really thought we had something. We have evidence of him being involved in the disappearance of a young witch."

I swallowed as unease shifted through me. "I didn't know that."

"Of course, you didn't. You don't work for me. That evidence was stored securely with Angel Force. No one gets in and out of the evidence room unless they're authorized to do so. It's a secure system. Somehow, Isaac knew exactly where he needed to target to get the evidence."

I scrubbed a hand down my face. "What happened to the witch who went missing? Did you find her?"

Dazielle pursed her lips. "We found part of her."

I winced and closed my eyes for a second. "Okay, confession time. But before you berate me, I did this all in a good cause."

"You admit to meeting with Isaac?"

"I do. I was out of Willow Tree Falls, hunting a demon. We arranged to meet. Isaac told me that he had information about the whereabouts of my dad."

"Tempest." Dazielle hissed out air. "Of course, you're not going to resist that. And when you met Isaac, he wanted information about Angel Force."

I nodded. "It seemed like a reasonable exchange. He wanted to know the layout of the building and where the evidence room was. He assured me it would be a swift in and out job. I'm surprised you even realized the evidence was missing."

"There were two very obvious clues that showed me there'd been a break-in," Dazielle said.

"The feather was one clue. Not the smartest of moves leaving that behind. What else alerted you?"

"Oriel and her injuries."

"Who's Oriel?"

"One of my angels who was almost killed by your selfish act."

I slid her a glance. "What are you talking about? How was she injured?"

"Oriel's been working in the evidence room for twenty years."

"Hold on! There's an angel who works here that I haven't met? I know all your angels. What do you do, keep her chained to the desk so she can't leave?"

"I don't keep her chained anywhere," Dazielle said. "Oriel's obsessed with ensuring the preservation of evidence. It's what she lives for. Out of choice, she hasn't set foot out of Angel Force since she began working here. And wide-open spaces make her jumpy. She enjoys the calm quiet of the evidence room."

"She's an angel! Angels love to fly in wide-open spaces."

"Not this one."

"Where does she sleep? Does she shower? What does she do for food? And what about sunlight? Surely, she must need to stretch her wings. How does—"

"Enough! It's her choice. Oriel gets her food sent to her, she sleeps in the evidence room, and there are on-site facilities, so she can deal with all her hygiene needs as required."

I groaned as the realization hit me. "Oriel was sleeping in the evidence room when Isaac broke in?"

"Exactly. And he wasn't expecting that. He struck in the early hours of the morning, when I assume he expected the place to be empty. Oriel must have disturbed him and put up a fight."

"And Isaac struck back?"

"It's hard to tell. Oriel was injured by falling masonry."

"How's she doing?"

"Not good," Dazielle said. "She hasn't regained consciousness since the attack, which was three weeks ago."

I rubbed a finger up and down my forehead. "What did Isaac do to her?"

"If the blown apart wall didn't get her, he must have given her a hard whack on the head. We won't know until she wakes up."

"She's been out of it for three weeks?"

Dazielle nodded. "She's got a bed in the hospital, which is where she'll stay until she opens her eyes and we can talk to her."

Guilt gripped my stomach. Isaac had promised me this wouldn't happen. No one was supposed to get hurt. "I should send her a fruit basket or maybe some muffins. Make it up to her."

"You should definitely do something." Dazielle sighed. "I should have you arrested for your part in this."

"I didn't think this would happen. I didn't know about Oriel," I said. "Isaac played down how important the evidence was. And, well, I was desperate for information. I knew if anyone could find something useful about what happened to my dad, it would be him."

She glared at me before shaking her head. "And did Isaac get you what you needed?"

"He got me a lead, not a great one. But it's the best information I've had so far. Isaac also got me questioning a few things about my dad. It's a messed-up situation, which I'm still trying to untangle."

Dazielle walked around behind my chair. She placed a hand on my shoulder. Any second now, she would crush me between her wings. Maybe I should let her. I'd gotten one of her angel's badly injured and valuable evidence stolen to fulfill my own self-seeking needs.

Instead, she simply squeezed hard. "I am tempted to arrest you, but given the mitigating circumstances, you're getting a stern warning to steer clear. No more investigating. Not in this case or any future investigations. If you're going to share information about the work we do here, I can't trust you around my angels."

Her hand vanished from my shoulder as she walked back in front of me.

"You can trust me," I said. "I did it because I was desperate."

"And what's to say you won't be desperate again? Maybe another member of your family will need help, and the only person offering to assist you demands inside information about my angels. You can't be relied on."

That hurt more than it should. It felt like a punch in the gut. As much as I protested, I sort of liked helping the angels figure out these mysteries. "You want me to stop investigating Bathsheba's murder, even though I think the guys you're holding are innocent?"

Dazielle nodded. "I absolutely do. Stay away from this case. We've got enough going on without having to keep an eye on what you're doing."

I tipped my head back and stared at the ceiling. Mack and Coleman were too obvious as targets, and they were weak magic users. Dazielle's head had been turned toward the chaos in the village. She thought this was an easy case to solve. What if it wasn't that easy?

"Tempest, this is your one and only warning. Stay away from this. Keep your head down, and I may forget that you caused me so much trouble with that break-in," Dazielle said.

My mouth turned down, but I nodded. "I'll stay out of your way."

However, if I happened to bump into one of the suspects on my list for Bathsheba's murder, there'd be no harm in me having a friendly chat with them.

I just needed to forget to mention that to Dazielle.

Chapter 9

By the time I left Angel Force, the dark clouds had moved in. The village had a gloomy, oppressive feel to it. The temperature had also dropped, making my skin goosebump. Thunder rumbled around us as I walked with Wiggles back to the center of the village.

The atmosphere crackled with tension, and the hairs on my arms stood up. Several of the stores already had their closed signs up, which was unusual.

"I take it things weren't too friendly with Dazielle," Wiggles said.

"You could say that," I said. "We've been well and truly warned off this case."

"Which means we're going to keep investigating."

"Sure. But we need to be discreet," I said. "Before we do that, I need something to make me smile again."

"Doughnuts?" Wiggles suggested.

"I'm in the mood for cupcakes. Lots of cupcakes." I headed to Sprinkles and frowned when I spotted the closed sign. I checked the time. It was still two hours before official closing.

I peered through the window, but there was no one inside. The lights were off, the cabinets empty of the delicious sugary treats I longed for. It looked like it had been empty for hours.

I tugged at my bottom lip. "Where's Patti?"

"Maybe she's with that woman whose hair was on fire," Wiggles said. "I wonder what she did to make Patti set her alight."

"I doubt that was Patti. Dazielle said the whole village is being a bit freaky."

"How about Unicorn's Trough?" Wiggles turned tail and marched past the stores.

"Why not?" I'd been popping in to see Brogan Costin since he returned from his trip away, following the spectacular fail of his last relationship. His girlfriend had turned out to be a cheat who pretended to be a demon to scare her husband. Brogan was having a tough time getting over that. Anyone would.

We strode along the quiet street until we came to the café.

I walked through the door to find the place almost deserted, apart from one customer who sipped coffee as he stared out the window.

Brogan strolled out of the back room, and a frown darkened his attractive features. "I'm about to close."

"Then my timing's perfect," I said brightly. "We're in need of cupcakes."

He jerked his chin up. "How many?"

"A dozen," I said. "No, make that two dozen." Maybe a big order might cheer up Brogan. He'd always had an intense character, but it had slipped into downright surly since his relationship failed. Maybe he blamed me for what had happened, but I hadn't been the one who'd knocked a wall on his cheating girlfriend's head.

"I only have chocolate and vanilla," he said.

"Perfect."

Brogan shrugged a shoulder. "Fine."

"Have you seen the weirdness going on around the village?" I asked.

"I've noticed a severe lack of customers if that's what you mean." He shoveled the cupcakes less than gently into a box, smearing the frosting as he did so.

"Um, not really. It is quiet in here today, though. And what about this weather? A storm's gathering."

"Good hunting weather," he muttered.

Oh boy, he wasn't making this easy. "Speaking of hunting, how are your grandparents doing?"

He flashed his fangs at me. "Let's not talk about them, shall we?"

The last I'd heard about his grandparents, the actual killers of his cheating girlfriend, they were being interviewed by the Vampire Council to determine their punishment.

"Give them my best," I said.

"Yeah, I'm sure they'll appreciate that." He rang up my sale. "Anything else?"

"Maybe one of your delightful smiles."

"I'm all out of those," he said. "There's no point in smiling anymore."

I handed over the money, grabbed the cupcakes, and left. Brogan was in no mood to play nice today, and I was done trying to be friendly.

As I walked out of Unicorn's Trough and had the door rudely slammed shut behind me, I spotted Liam, Charlotte, and Picasso up ahead.

I hurried to catch up with them. "Liam, how are you doing?"

He turned, and his gaze ran over me before he nodded. "As you can imagine, this is a difficult time for all of us."

"I'm sure it is," I said. "I am sorry about what happened to Bathsheba. Where did you stay last night?"

"In our hospitality suite," he said.

I stared at him. "You mean the tent? Where Bathsheba was killed?"

He shook his head. "We have separate areas for sleeping. The angels asked that the crime scene remain undisturbed, but they allowed us to sleep there."

I wouldn't be all that comfortable sleeping at a murder scene.

"We must get on." He gestured for Charlotte and Picasso to move.

"Of course." I hurried to keep up as they strode toward the stone circle. "You must have seen everything that happened in the tent. You were standing beside your wife when the attack happened."

"Not exactly," he said. "Listen, Tempest, is it?"

I nodded. "That's right."

"This is a time for the family to be together. We're all in shock over what happened to Bathsheba and dealing with our grief."

"I get that. And I don't mean to intrude."

"Then don't," he said. "We've got things to figure out over the next few days."

"Does that include the arrival of your new sister?" I looked at Picasso and Charlotte.

Charlotte glanced at her brother. "How do you know about Lucy?"

"Fanny mentioned her to me," I said. "She said Bathsheba was thinking of retiring from the touring circuit, so she could spend more time with her new arrival. Will she still join you?"

"Of course not." Charlotte's lips pursed. "She'll need to find another home. Lucy won't want to join us now. Good thing too."

That sounded a lot like jealousy to me. "You don't want a new sister?"

"Tempest, this isn't a good time." Liam shook his head and sighed. "Now wouldn't be the right moment to bring someone new into the family. We'll have a long period of adjustment as we find our feet without Bathsheba. A new child wouldn't be appropriate."

"It was what Mom wanted," Picasso mumbled. "She always said she loved having her children around her."

"That's not happening now," Charlotte said. "It's just the two of us. We're fine as we are. It's better this way."

"Why is that?" I asked.

Charlotte huffed out a breath. "Mom's dead. We don't know what we're doing next. Do you think bringing some damaged child from the care system into this muddle would be good for her?"

"Um, no, I guess not."

"We just want to leave this place," Liam said, "but the angels have asked that we stay until they charge the killers. I don't understand why they can't get on with it. I was informed this morning that they still haven't confessed."

"Did any of you actually see Mack or Coleman shoot that magic at Bathsheba?" I asked.

Liam stopped walking and turned to me. "No, but we heard strange noises, then two men appeared in front of Bathsheba and demanded her jewels."

"And they got in through a back door?" I asked.

"They must have," Liam said.

"Of course, Mommy protested," Charlotte said. "She wanted to fight back, but—"

Liam patted her arm. "I told her not to. I was worried for her safety. You can replace diamonds. You can't replace the love of your life." He looked away.

Charlotte and Picasso looked at each other and raised their eyebrows.

"What happened next?" I asked.

"I told Bathsheba to hand over her jewels," Liam said. "She wasn't happy, but she did it."

"That's when the robbers triggered the blackout spell," Picasso said softly.

"And it was definitely them who triggered that spell?" I asked.

"Yes!" Liam said. "The hospitality suite was plunged into blackness, and there was this blinding flash of light. That was the spell that killed Bathsheba. There was a scuffling sound, which must have been the men escaping, and I got this awful smell of burning filling my nose. I didn't know what it was until you came in and triggered a light spell. Then I saw, well, you were there. You know what happened."

"Did Coleman and Mack attack you because you tried to fight them?" I asked Picasso. "Is that when you were hit in the arm?"

"No, I didn't move from my seat," he said. "Charlotte had hold of my hand tightly, and she was shaking. I could tell she was terrified. I stayed by her side to keep her safe. Of course, if they'd come at her, I'd have protected her."

"It was a wild shot in the dark that got you?" I asked. "They could have been aiming at anybody."

"I suppose so," Picasso said. "I got lucky. It was a flesh wound. It's already healed, thanks to a few spells."

"You were fortunate," Liam said. "I was standing right next to Bathsheba and felt the power of the spell as it slammed into her. I was almost knocked off my feet. That must have been what made me faint."

"Yes, that would be it." I tried not to sound sarcastic. I had a feeling Liam would be worse than useless in a real fight.

"Those men meant to kill Bathsheba," Liam said. "This attack was calculated. They knew where she'd be and what jewels she had on her."

"How would they know that?" I asked. "Unless they've been following you to see what she was carrying. How would they know it would be worth robbing her when she performed here?"

"They must have seen her perform at another venue," Charlotte said. "Mommy never goes on stage unless she's dressed in her finest clothes and jewels. She loves to put on a performance and dazzle everyone. Maybe they saw her at a previous venue or saw old promotional materials. She always wore her best jewels when she had her picture taken."

"You think they waited until she did her next public performance before they struck?" I asked.

"That must be it," Liam said. "They followed us to Willow Tree Falls. They knew what they were doing."

"Yet they're not powerful," I said. "They aren't masters at spell casting."

Charlotte dabbed at her eyes. "I can't understand why they did it. They have no conscience. They're monsters."

Picasso wrapped an arm around his sister's shoulders. "It's okay. They'll get what's coming to them."

"We really need to go," Liam said. "We're exhausted after everything that has happened, and we need to speak to the angels again to get an update. Hopefully, they'll have charged those men, and we'll be able to leave tomorrow."

"I'd just like to ask you—"

"No more." Liam held up his hand. "This is a horrible time for us all. We need some space."

I took a step back. They did look exhausted. I should stop pushing, but I still wasn't convinced that Mack and Coleman murdered Bathsheba. Could the robbery have been a set-up? A cover for murder?

Liam nodded at me before turning and ushering Charlotte and Picasso away.

"They're hiding something," I said. "Did you see the look that passed between Charlotte and Picasso when Liam talked about how much he loved Bathsheba?"

Wiggles nodded. "That man is a terrible liar."

"Something doesn't add up in that relationship. We need to find out what the problem is and if it had anything to do with Bathsheba's murder."

"But first, cupcakes," Wiggles said.

I grinned. "Of course. We've always got time for cupcakes."

Chapter 10

I'd just flicked open the locks on the front door of Cloven Hoof when it was shoved open, and I was almost smacked on the nose.

Aurora rushed through the door, her green hair a fuzzy mess around her face and mascara streaked down her cheeks. "You're here!"

"Where else would I be? It's opening time. What's up?"

She lifted a bundle of blankets in her arms. "It's Bandit."

I peered into the blankets. Nestled right in the middle was the cat. "She's still no better?"

"She's worse." Aurora hurried through into the bar, clutching Bandit against her chest. "She alternates between being too hot and then too cold. And she's flickering with magic."

"Bring her over here." I hurried to a booth, and we settled on the seats before Aurora placed the bundled-up Bandit on the table.

"I don't know what to do to help her," Aurora said. "I've tried everything I can think of. Nothing helps."

"Did you take her to see Abigail at Fur Babies?" I lifted the corner of the blanket, and Bandit growled at me.

"I did. She was helpful but doesn't know what's wrong. Because Bandit's not a true familiar, Abigail doesn't have much experience with what might be causing her illness. She gave me several spells to try and a few herbal remedies, but I've tried most of those already. I don't think my magic is strong enough to make her better."

"You have plenty of strong healing magic. It's what you're good at."

"Not since the village magic went out of control. I tried a basic spell of warmth and set fire to things. I'm scared to try too many spells in case I make Bandit worse."

I risked touching the top of Bandit's head. She was blazing hot, her skin sticky. "When did she last eat?"

"She's had nothing for twenty-four hours," Aurora said. "Bandit never likes to go more than three hours without having a snack. She says she gets weak if she doesn't eat at regular intervals."

Customers walked through the door of the club and headed to the bar.

"We can't keep her down here. A sickly cat will put off the clientele. Bring Bandit up to the apartment," I said.

Aurora's bottom lip trembled as she carefully picked up Bandit and snuggled her against her chest. "We need to make her better. I don't know how I'll cope if anything bad happens to her."

"We will." As I walked past the bar with Aurora, I nodded at Merrie. "I'll be upstairs if you need me."

She nodded and waved me away as she served drinks.

We headed up the stairs into the quiet of my apartment.

Wiggles raised his head from where he lay sprawled on the couch. He stared at the blankets, and his eyes glowed red. "Something stinks."

"Shush. Don't be rude. Bandit's very sensitive right now." Aurora perched on the couch and carefully arranged the blanket on her knees.

Wiggles sniffed the blanket and recoiled. "She smells terrible. What have you been feeding her?"

"Nothing! That's a part of the problem. Bandit's not eating." Aurora's eyes filled with tears.

Wiggles' nose wrinkled before he took another tentative sniff. "She really smells weird. Not like a cat. They always have that hot, furry whiff about them. I've gotten used to it. This is different. It smells like... I'm not sure. Nothing good."

Aurora's wide, tear-filled eyes went to me. "If we combine our magic, it might help. We're stronger together."

"It's worth a shot," I said. "What spells have you used on her so far?" I walked over to my bookcase and pulled out two spell books before settling on the couch next to Aurora.

"A calm spell, three physical healing spells. I even tried a removal spell. I wondered if some entity had infected Bandit and was making her sick."

I flicked through the first spell book on my knees. "You think she was possessed by some malevolent spirit and that's why she's all hot and freaky smelling?"

"She already has a malevolent spirit," Wiggles said. "Cats are the antichrist."

Aurora glared at him. "They're not. Cats are adorable, especially my baby."

"As adorable as me?" Wiggles wagged his stubby tail.

"I won't think you're adorable at all if you keep bad-mouthing my kitty," she said. She gave Wiggles' head a brief pet.

"Place Bandit on the couch between us," I said, "and unwrap that blanket. I can feel the heat radiating off her from here."

Aurora eased Bandit off her lap.

Bandit lay panting on her side, her tongue out. Clouds of fur drifted from her body.

"Hey! She's shedding all over my favorite couch," Wiggles said. "That'll have to be cleaned. I can't sleep surrounded by sick cat stink."

"That's been happening all day," Aurora said. "If I brush her, I get loads of fur. That's not normal."

"It's definitely not." I watched a clump of ginger fur float through the air.

Wiggles backed up. "You don't think this is contagious, do you? Am I going to get sick too?"

"Whatever it is, I think you're immune," I said. "If it was something she could spread to other people, you'd have caught it by now."

"Maybe the symptoms don't show for a few days." Wiggles coughed. "Actually, I am feeling warm. And I had a weird dream about a huge piece of cheese."

"I don't know about the cheese, but you're a hellhound. Warm is your default setting." I eyed him carefully. "Do you really feel bad?"

He snuffled around in his fur for a few seconds. "I'm good. Even so, I'm moving into the bedroom." Wiggles hopped off the couch and trotted away. When he reached my bedroom door, he glanced back at Bandit, concern clear on his face. As much as he tried to deny it, he'd developed a soft spot for this prickly, pungent cat.

I passed my hand slowly across Bandit's side. Something crackled against my skin and a faint light flared. "Did you see that?" I moved closer.

Aurora leaned over Bandit, bumping her head against mine. "What is it? Some sort of virus?"

I moved my hand over Bandit again and got the same response. "I've never seen a virus like that."

Bandit squirmed as if our close inspection made her uncomfortable.

I blinked and jerked my head back before scrubbing my eyes.

"What? Did you see something bad?" Aurora licked her lips. "Tell me."

"It's weird. For a second, I thought I saw a wing coming out of her side."

"A wing!" Aurora stared at Bandit. "I don't see it. Are you sure?"

"Nope. But it looked like she was trying to shift forms."

"Bandit can't change form. She's my familiar." Aurora sniffed back her tears. "I've gotten used to her being around."

I scrubbed my forehead. "You have to remember she's not always been a cat. Maybe this is a side effect of the spell that was cast on her. The magic could be finally wearing off."

"Do you think I'm going to lose Bandit?" Aurora's voice wobbled. "I... I don't want that to happen. She's my friend."

"She's your friend who's in a lot of trouble." I hated seeing my sister so sad. She'd had a rough time with her deceitful fiancé. Bandit, for all her sass, had helped her to heal and open the door to new adventures. "Let's try this healing spell for curing general malaise I found. That could help."

"Yes! We must get Bandit well." Aurora reached over and caught hold of my hand. When our magic joined, it doubled in strength. Aurora's magic had a light, almost tickling sensation to it as it flowed across my fingers, joining with my slightly darker, hotter magic.

The healing spell flowed out of our fingers and wrapped around Bandit in a spiral of soft pink haze.

We stayed seated for several minutes, our magic entwined, concentrating hard on removing whatever was wrong with Bandit.

"I think it's working," Aurora whispered. "Her legs have stopped twitching."

I slowly pulled back the spell and shook out my fingers. "Let's try a few more spells while we're here. We need to keep her calm. We also need to get her to start eating and drinking again."

"How about an energy spell?" Aurora asked. "Maybe she simply needs a boost."

"A sleep spell might be better," I said. "She's been restless for a couple of days, and she's probably exhausted. We don't want to fill her with artificial juice only to have her crash later. Let's focus on keeping her calm and getting her temperature down. Maybe then she'll wake up and feel like eating something."

After a spell of sleep, a spell of cold to help reduce her temperature, and a spell of calm, Bandit was finally resting and appeared to be in a deep sleep. She'd stopped panting, and her fur was no longer falling out.

Aurora let out a huge sigh and leaned over to give me a tight hug. "Thanks. I knew you'd be able to help."

"Is it safe to come out?" Wiggles trotted out of the bedroom. "How's the annoying furball doing?"

"A little better," I said. "Don't disturb her. She needs to rest."

"I'm not going anywhere near something that smells of three-day-old socks left out in the midday sun," Wiggles said. "It's put me right off my dinner."

"You've already eaten," I said.

"I meant my second dinner."

I shook my head. "Let's leave Bandit for now. You never know, she might wake up after a while." I stood, made us both hot chocolates with marshmallows on top, and returned to the couch, passing a full mug to Aurora.

"How's everything going with the investigation into Bathsheba's murder?" Aurora curled her feet under her, her gaze resting on Bandit.

"I want to speak to her children when they're on their own," I said. "I bumped into Liam, Charlotte, and Picasso earlier today. It's definitely not all happy families."

Aurora set her mug down. "I heard an interesting rumor about Liam in the store today."

I leaned closer. "What was that?"

"People are saying that Bathsheba was openly looking for husband number five. She even made an announcement in a live interview that she needed a fresh start."

My mouth dropped open. "They've been married less than two years. She couldn't have been bored with him already."

"It sounds like that's exactly what she was." Aurora's blue eyes glittered. "And someone else told me that there's an airtight prenuptial agreement. Bathsheba had one in place for all her previous husbands, apart from the first one. He left her when she got famous and took a huge cut of her earnings. She vowed never to do anything so foolish again. Anyone who married Bathsheba had to sign a prenuptial agreement. If they leave her or cheat on her, they get nothing. If she leaves them, they get a small annual allowance, but that's it."

"How do you know all this?"

"It's out there in the public domain. Bathsheba Delaware was hugely famous. Therefore, her private life was of interest to a lot of people. She did a ton of interviews talking about her marriages."

"I bet Liam gets something if Bathsheba died while they were married. That's a good motive for murder. Do your information sources have anything to say about that?"

Aurora shrugged. "I'm not sure what he'd be entitled to. He could inherit everything now she's dead. That's often what happens when one half of a married couple dies. Everything goes to the surviving partner."

"Liam must only be about ten years older than Charlotte and Picasso. He's got a lot of living left to do."

"And will do it in style if he gets the bulk of the estate. Bathsheba clearly liked her younger men." Aurora flashed her eyebrows. "I'm into the more mature companion."

"And how are things going with Lex?"

She grinned and ducked her head. "I'm taking it slowly. We're still getting to know each other."

"Just in case he's hiding any more dead wives in the closet?"

She smacked my arm not too gently. "No! Lex didn't know his wife had faked her own death. There aren't any secrets between us."

"So, he's shown you where he keeps his hoard of gold and his genie wish lamp?" I couldn't resist a bit of gently teasing.

"Shush! Enough of that, or you'll disturb Bandit." Aurora plumped a cushion behind her. "He's a decent man. Kind and thoughtful and not pushing for anything. I like him."

"Then I'm happy for you." I downed half my mug of hot chocolate and scooped the marshmallows off the top with a finger. "Getting back to Bathsheba's unusual family, I didn't get a sense they liked each other. It felt more like they were tolerating being with each other because they were stuck in this uncomfortable situation. I also mentioned about Bathsheba adopting a new daughter. Fanny told me about that. They dismissed it and said it wasn't an option. None of them were keen on welcoming a new member of the family. It suggests that family unit won't remain intact for much longer."

"Maybe only Bathsheba was interested in having another child," Aurora said. "Now she's gone, it means they don't have to split their inheritance with anyone else if the child doesn't join them."

"Which is another good reason for killing Bathsheba now," I said. "It means her assets only get split three ways instead of four."

"You think one of them did it?" Aurora said.

"Not for certain. I'm actually leaning toward Fanny rather than a family member. She hated Bathsheba and had an opportunity to sneak into the tent and blast that spell at her."

Aurora stroked a hand gently down Bandit's back. "What's your next move to uncover the truth?"

"I want to get Liam and the children on their own, speak to them separately. The trouble is, as soon as the angels charge Mack and Coleman with the murder, the family is leaving. I don't have much time left."

"From what I've heard, the angels have their hands full with all the weird things happening around the village. It might take them a while to process this case." Aurora ran a hand down her green hair.

"How's your store behaving?" I asked. "Dazielle said there have been problems everywhere."

"It's still being naughty. Everyone's magic is playing up, though. I'm not being targeted. Willow Tree Falls is unhappy."

"It must have something to do with this murder," I said. "It happened so close to the stone circle, and it wasn't long after that, that things went wrong. Remember how the stone circle was all sparkly and excited about the music?"

"Do you think the stones are grieving the loss of Bathsheba by jinxing everyone else?"

I shrugged. "The circle didn't seem all that impressed by Bathsheba. They didn't dance along while she performed. They adored Fanny, though. Maybe this is simply the stone circle coming down after its musical high."

"I don't know. They've never behaved like this before." Aurora looked out the window where dark clouds had amassed in a gloomy sky. "It looks more like the work of some demi-demon."

"The circle is full of an ancient powerful magic. I imagine it can do anything it wants when it puts its mind to it."

"The stones are showing us how unhappy they are," Aurora said. "They want this murder cleared up."

"It could be that they're acting up because they know the angels have the wrong people in custody. They want to make sure that Fanny, or whoever did it, is arrested."

"You should visit the stone circle. Ask them what they want."

"And get my head taken off by a rogue blast of magic?" I shook my head. "That task will go to the bottom of my to-do list, but I will swing by if they don't settle down soon. Maybe having a word with them will quieten things down."

"You definitely need to get this solved," Aurora said, "before the village explodes and I go bald. Green hair I can handle, so long as I have some hair."

I chuckled. "I'm getting used to you with green hair. It sort of clashes with your blue eyes, but it's trendy."

"I'll be happy when I can get back to blonde." Her bottom lip stuck out. "Every spell I try only lasts five minutes before the color fades and I become green again. It's not fair. Your hair hasn't changed color."

I stroked a strand of my dark locks through my fingers. "Not yet. I bet the stones will get around to me, eventually. And my club's on the other side of the village from the circle. I'm probably one of the farthest away from its influence. Maybe its power doesn't reach this far."

"The stones are affecting the weather. I'm sure they can send out magical tendrils to reach your club and mess with your hair color," Aurora said.

"Let's hope it doesn't come to that," I said. "First thing tomorrow, I'll head out and talk to the suspects in this murder and see if I can get anything to shake loose."

"Good plan." Aurora pressed her lips together. "And how are things going with the investigation into Dad?"

"There's nothing new." I sank back in my seat. "I've put feelers out to see if we can get any up-to-date information. Granny Dottie's doing the same."

"I'm still not convinced he was seen in the Dark Realm," Aurora said. "He wouldn't go there. He knows how dangerous that place is."

"If we don't get new information about him soon, the only option I see is going there and checking it out for myself."

Aurora shook her head. "It's too dangerous. I don't want to lose you as well."

I tilted my head, a tickle of sisterly love warming my heart. "You'll never lose me. I'm sticking around here for good."

She smiled. "I'm glad to hear it. You're my favorite sister."

"I'm also your only sister."

She giggled. "It's the same thing."

Bandit groaned and rolled onto her back, her legs kicking in the air.

"The magic can't already have faded," I said. "We pumped loads of spells into her."

"She looks like she already needs more," Aurora said, a frown marring her face. "If we keep going at this rate, we'll be exhausted and drained of magic."

Wiggles nudged his way onto my lap and glared down at Bandit. "Wake up, you lazy old thing. I need someone to poke fun at." He prodded her with a paw.

Bandit groaned again and flicked her tail in the air.

"You're not fooling anyone," Wiggles said. "You're faking this to get attention. You know I'm the favorite, so you'll use any trick to knock me off my pedestal."

Bandit's top lip curled.

"I think she can hear you," Aurora said.

"Maybe don't goad the seriously sick cat," I said to Wiggles. "She won't thank you when she gets better. You know how Bandit holds a grudge."

Wiggles puffed out a plume of sulfuric smoke. "She's not that ill. I bet she's not even really asleep."

"If that's true, then you definitely need to stop teasing her," I said. "Or she'll put cat nip in your food."

His nose wrinkled. "There are better ways to get attention. Take a leaf out of my book, Bandit. Make sure you're adorably cute and cuddly at all times. Then everyone loves you."

Aurora petted him on the head. "Of course, we love you, but I also love Bandit. I want her better."

I placed Wiggles back on the floor. "She'll be fine in a few days. Let's do more magic to get her back to sleep and settled."

We performed the same set of spells, but they didn't seem to take. Bandit squirmed and snarled as the magic drifted over her, not latching on and calming her like it had previously done.

"I should take her home. Maybe she'll be more settled in her cardboard box on the counter." Aurora tried to lift Bandit.

Bandit spun in her arms and growled, making it impossible for Aurora to keep hold of her.

Wiggles nudged my leg. "Cats and cardboard boxes, I never did get that obsession."

"It's a bit like you and pillows," I said.

"Ah! That makes sense."

"Ouch! Get your claws out of my arm." Aurora extracted Bandit's front claws from her forearm, placed her swiftly on the couch, and inspected the bloody pinpricks in her skin.

"She's not happy about being moved," I said.

Bandit spat, and a low growl rumbled in her chest. Her claws flashed in the air as she looked for a target to attach to and cause maximum damage.

Thunder rumbled around the building, and an arc of lightning lit the sky.

"It could be the weather unsettling her." Aurora looked out the window. "I'm not a big fan of storms. It looks like one's about to set in."

"Stay here for the night if you want to," I said.

"I don't want to be any bother," Aurora said.

"Bandit does," Wiggles said. "She's loving this."

"You're only jealous," I said.

"Of that flea-bitten thing? Not a chance." He stomped away, muttering under his breath.

"Both of you stay here," I said to Aurora. "We can keep an eye on Bandit and alternate trying different healing spells. Something will stick. When it does, she'll recover and then you can go back home."

"Thanks. That's a great idea. We'll fix her between us." Aurora looked down at Bandit, who was still swiping her paws at an invisible enemy.

Rain lashed against the apartment window as lightning crackled across the sky. Whatever was going wrong with the magic in Willow Tree Falls, it needed fixing and fast. I still had a murder to solve, and I didn't want to do it while trudging through the pouring rain at risk of being lightning struck at any second.

Fix Bandit, placate the stones, and solve a murder. Those were on the top of my to-do list for tomorrow.

Chapter 11

I yawned as I rolled out of bed the next morning. I was surprised that Wiggles wasn't sprawled out next to me. He usually managed to steal at least one of my pillows, and I'd wake to find him with it squashed between his legs, a look of happy abandonment on his furry face. But he was nowhere to be seen.

I shoved my feet into my slippers and stumbled out into the lounge.

Wiggles sat by the couch, his nose resting on the edge of the cushion as he looked at Bandit.

"How's she doing?" I asked.

He jerked back and looked around, a guilty expression on his face. "How would I know?"

I smirked at him. "Because you've been watching her. I know you've got a soft spot for Bandit."

"That's not true," he said. "I just didn't want her turning into a psycho cat and slaughtering everyone in their sleep. I don't trust her. What's for breakfast?" He trotted into the kitchen after me, glancing back at Bandit as he did so.

"How thoughtful of you. How about some yummy dog kibble?" I shook the sack of game and greens vegetable dry mix.

He shook his head. "After the night I've had, I need a pancake stack."

"What was wrong with your night?" I switched on the kettle as I rubbed the sleep out of my eyes.

"You didn't hear the thunderstorm? It raged most of the night."

"The music was too loud in the club to hear anything after I went downstairs," I said. "When I came to bed, I did a few more spells on Bandit and then collapsed. I didn't hear a thing."

"Well, between worrying that I was about to pick up something infectious from that mangy cat on the couch and ducking every time there was a clap of thunder, I've had barely any sleep," Wiggles said. "I'll age prematurely if I have too many more nights like that."

A glance out the window suggested the freaky weather wasn't done with us just yet. Huge yellow clouds glowered back at me, and lightning flickered in the distance.

"Where's Aurora?" I hunted through the cupboard for suitable ingredients to make pancakes. All I had was some cornmeal, marshmallows, and a tub of dark chocolate chips. I'd used all my pancake supplies and had yet to re-stock.

"In the shower," Wiggles said.

The door to the bathroom opened. Aurora emerged encased in two fluffy blue towels, one wrapped around her hair. "Morning."

I nodded at her. "Coffee?"

"Yes, please. Make mine a strong one." She hurried over to the couch and sat next to Bandit. "She's a little better. Her eyes opened for a while last night not long after you came back from the club and did those spells on her."

I left the coffee making and walked over to Bandit. I pressed a hand against her head. "She feels cooler."

"Which is a good sign." Aurora wiggled her fingers at me. "Have you got enough juice left to give her another healing spell?"

I did have that bone-weary ache that meant my magic was drained, but I could manage a few simple healing spells. "Sure, why not?" I linked my fingers and stretched out my arms.

We sat on the couch, me smelling like I'd just rolled out of bed and not brushed my teeth, and Aurora smelling of my coconut shampoo and minty toothpaste, and performed several healing spells one after the other on Bandit.

She jerked a few times, her paws spinning through the air. Suddenly, her eyes flicked open, and she flopped onto her belly.

Aurora lowered her hand, a gasp of delight flying from her mouth. "Bandit! Are you awake?"

Bandit flicked her eyes up to Aurora's face. "Ugh! Where am I?"

Aurora grinned and clapped her hands together. "Tempest's apartment. We've been doing spells on you all night. How are you?"

She sniffed the air. "Spells? Why? And why do I smell hellhound close by?"

Wiggles' head appeared around the side of the couch. "That would be my delightful odor you're experiencing."

Bandit groaned. "No wonder I feel so unwell if I've spent the night here with that furry stink bomb."

"Wiggles has nothing to do with you being ill," Aurora said. "You've been really sick. What's the last thing you remember?"

Bandit didn't move, only her tail flicking slightly from side to side. "I remember you leaving to see the singer at the stone circle. It was dark, and I felt really tired. I figured I'd just have an early night, and that's all I remember."

"You don't recall anything since then?" Aurora said.

"I occasionally felt a bit buzzed." Bandit glared at Wiggles. "Was that you?"

"It wasn't Wiggles," Aurora said. "I've been trying different spells on you. Abigail had a go as well, but when you got really bad last night, I brought you to Tempest."

Bandit sniffed again. "Huh! Okay. I'm hungry."

"Of course! You must be starving." Aurora jumped up. "Tempest, have you got any fruit?"

I glanced at my sad looking fruit basket with its wrinkled apples. "Not really. You're welcome to anything that hasn't gone off."

Aurora raced into the kitchen. She cut up an apple before returning to the couch and carefully hand feeding Bandit.

"I'm sure she can feed herself," Wiggles muttered.

"I'd do the same for you if you were feeling poorly," Aurora said.

Bandit polished off the apple. While she ate, her gaze kept flicking to me.

"What is it?" I asked.

Her whiskers twitched. "I feel like I need to tell you something important."

"Like what?"

"I forget," Bandit said. "It's epic, though. I just know it."

Wiggles burped. "Pardon me."

I wafted my hand in front of my face. "Buddy, you're smelling particularly ripe today. Is your magic okay? You're not going on the fritz because of the stone circle, are you?"

"It's... fine." He burped again, and flames flickered out of his mouth. "Maybe it's a little off. I've been feeling an intense desire to burn everything I look at. I figured it was having to put up with Bandit being on my couch that put me in a bad mood."

"It's the stone circle's influence," Aurora said. "It must be influencing your magic too."

"What's this about the stone circle?" Bandit asked.

"We're thinking the stone circle is angry because one of the singers was murdered next to it," I said. "Ever since she died, everyone's magic has been misfiring."

"Hold on. Someone's been killed, and the stone circle has gone gaga? Honestly, I get sick for a couple of days, and this place falls apart." Bandit shook her head.

"I'm wondering if that's what's causing your sickness," Aurora said. "Could the stones be making you unwell?"

"It's possible. I'm an extremely rare magical creature," Bandit said. "Something as ancient and important as the stone circle is bound to focus on me. I'm possibly one of a kind."

"Rare, my behind," Wiggles said. "You're a common, everyday house cat."

"Can an everyday house cat do this?" She weakly swiped a paw in the air.

"Of course." Wiggles barked out a laugh.

Bandit grunted. "Or this?" She tried to stand, but after a few seconds of struggling, flopped back on her belly.

"Easily." Wiggles blew out some pungent smoke. "Kitty, you need to work on your moves."

"Don't forget I have a side order of mystical being hidden under this fur," Bandit said.

"That could be why the stone circle is affecting you so badly," Aurora said. "You already had strong magic influencing you."

A fireball shot out of Wiggles' mouth and set light to the corner of Bandit's blanket.

I patted the flames out with the back of a spell book. "Wiggles, maybe you need to go cool off somewhere else."

"It's not me!" he said. "I didn't do that deliberately. It just happened."

"It's your subconscious making you act," Bandit said. "I always knew you didn't like me. You're probably really unhappy that I'm feeling better."

"I never pretended to like you. And you are hogging all the attention," he said.

"Wiggles, that's enough," I said.

Smoke drifted out of his nose. "It's not my fault. She makes me angry."

"Take your misfiring magic and your anger issues into the kitchen and have a hunt around for some food. You always get grumpy when you're hungry."

He stamped away on his stubby paws, grumbling to himself.

Bandit returned to staring at me. "I wish I could remember what it was I needed to tell you. I feel like it's life changing."

"For you or me?" I asked.

"Maybe for both of us." Bandit's ear flicked back. "It's like I'm holding onto this big secret, and it needs to come out. Every time I reach for it, it drifts away."

"Crazy cat," Wiggles mumbled from the kitchen.

"Do you feel up to going back home?" Aurora asked. "We've taken up enough of Tempest's time. She's got a murder she needs to look into."

"So long as you carry me," Bandit said. "I'm too weak to walk."

That comment earned her more grumbling complaints from Wiggles as he stuck his head in the trash can.

"I'll get dressed and walk back with you," I said. "I was going to make breakfast, but I'm missing half the ingredients, and Wiggles is demanding pancakes this morning."

"Great. It'll be good to see how my store has fared overnight."

"What's wrong with the store?" Bandit asked.

"More magical hijinks," Aurora said. "You've missed a lot."

I dashed around, had a quick wash, threw on some clothes, and we were ready to leave fifteen minutes later.

As I walked through the village with Aurora, Bandit, who was snuggled in her giant purse, and Wiggles, there were clear signs that everyone's magic had been misfiring overnight. Huge puddles of muddy water covered the ground, there were scorch marks on several of the buildings, and even a few trees had fallen. Red smoke drifted out of many of the chimney stacks.

"I don't like the look of this," Aurora said.

I shook my head. "Everything seems quiet now."

"Because most people are asleep," Aurora said. "Wait until everyone wakes up and the stone circle gets them again."

"Maybe the stones simply needed a day to get things off their chest. Hopefully, everything will be back to normal today." Although from the weird smoggy air around us, nothing felt quite as it should.

We arrived at Aurora's store door. Everything looked quiet inside. There were no smoking spells, flying books, or glowing crystals.

After she let us in, we had a good look around to ensure there were no unwelcome surprises waiting to attack.

"I think it's all good." She set Bandit on the counter. "I can handle things from here."

We said our goodbyes, and I headed out with Wiggles.

"We should eat before we do anything heroic," he said. "I'm still owed a stack of pancakes. Maybe even two stacks, given I had that evil feline in the apartment all night."

"We'll get to the pancakes soon enough." I slowed, and my eyebrows shot up. Liam was skulking out of the village hotel. What was he doing there? He was supposed to be staying in that fancy tent with Charlotte and Picasso.

A few seconds later, Fanny ran out the front door and handed him something. She touched his cheek before turning and dashing back inside.

"Do you think those two are together?" I asked Wiggles.

"They sure looked friendly to me," he said. "Now, about those pancakes."

I shook my head. "I wonder if Bathsheba knew about their relationship."

Wiggles sighed. "I doubt she'd have let it carry on if she'd figured out the stud muffin husband and her biggest rival were having naked fun together. I'm thinking pecan, maple syrup, and sugar sprinkles on my pancakes."

"What a reason to kill her," I said. "Fanny could have panicked if she thought that Bathsheba was onto them. She had to kill her before the truth came out and Liam was kicked out of the marital home with nothing but the shirt on those broad, manly shoulders. Aurora said the pre-nup listed cheating as a reason Liam would get nothing."

"Or Liam did it," Wiggles said. "His mistress might have egged him on. Ooh! That's an idea. We could have eggs before our pancakes. Poached on hot buttered toast."

"Let's see what he has to say for himself." I raced after Liam and called out to him just as he was about to head up the hill to the stone circle.

He didn't respond.

I raised my voice and hollered loud enough to wake the dead. "Liam, have you got a moment?"

He turned, and his lips pressed together as his gaze flashed back to the hotel. "Not really."

"I see you've moved out of the tent." I jogged up to him.

His eyes widened. "Of course not. I'm staying in our hospitality suite."

"Then it must have been your twin brother I saw coming out of the hotel with Fanny." I raised an eyebrow. "Is there something going on between you?"

His nostrils flared before his gaze drifted toward the village. "I'm not in an... easy situation right now."

"You sought comfort from Fanny? Did she offer you a sexy shoulder to cry on?"

He scrubbed the stubble on his chin. "You must understand, being married to somebody like Bathsheba came with a unique set of challenges."

"Challenges you must have been aware of when you entered into the marriage," I said.

He sighed. "Please, don't say anything about this to anyone. I'm not a cheater."

"Then tell me what's going on with you and Fanny."

His shoulders slumped, and he dragged a hand through his hair. "I tried so hard to make Bathsheba happy. I have an intense love for opera music and the talent of the singers. There's something about their passion and how they pour their emotions into their work that gets me hot. I'd been a devoted fan of Bathsheba's for years. I've seen dozens of her concerts. She noticed me one evening when I attended a show. I couldn't believe my luck when she singled me out at the end of the concert and asked me to have dinner with her."

"That's how you met?"

He nodded. "I was star struck. This beautiful, mature woman with a successful career and a following of millions wanted me. She used to put on private concerts for me. Everything was wonderful to begin with, providing I did everything she asked of me. And I was happy to oblige and delighted to be around such an incredible woman. I used to dismiss her quirks and her demands. After all, she was in the limelight all the time. She needed to have everything right, so she could give her best performance."

"I bet that got stale fast," I said. "Did the shine wear off when you realized how difficult it was to be married to such a demanding woman?"

His chin dropped to his chest. "When she got her own way, she was a delight to be around, but the second you questioned her, she turned mean and spiteful. And she had a vicious temper. She would lash out over the smallest thing. If a coffee wasn't the right temperature, or I was five minutes late picking up her favorite dinner. Something so small would send her into a tailspin. You can only put up with that for so long."

"But her privilege and position must have convinced you to stay, even though you weren't happy."

"I tried hard to see the positive in our relationship, but the money and all the glitzy places we visited soon wasn't enough to paper over the cracks. Bathsheba had this way of making you feel small and insignificant. She didn't treat me like a real husband. She had me on her arm and showed me around like I was another piece of her expensive jewelry. She did that to everyone. It makes you feel terrible. I'd had enough of feeling worthless."

"And then Fanny flashed those pretty eyes at you, and you just melted?"

His mouth tightened. "We've been friends for a long time. She's always been around, often supporting Bathsheba at events. And being on the same circuit, our paths crossed. Bathsheba was cruel to both of us. We bonded because of that."

"You're in love with Fanny?"

He nodded. "I was working up the courage to tell Bathsheba that I was leaving her. I didn't care about what I was leaving behind. I want to be with Fanny."

"Bathsheba found out about your plans?"

"Of course not. She was too self-absorbed to notice that things weren't right between us. She didn't love me. But she loved to brag about her young, gorgeous husband and all the things she made me do. I was a joke. It was humiliating. I know exactly what people think about me. Handsome but stupid. Bathsheba even said that to my face."

"And how fortunate that now you've got the perfect way out," I said. "Bathsheba's been murdered, and you're free to pursue your romance with Fanny."

He shook his head. "This is all such a mess, but I am relieved she's dead. I refuse to feel bad about this."

"Especially if you're going to inherit her fortune, now she's gone."

Liam snorted a laugh. "I wish. I don't get any big pay-out from her will. Bathsheba's not foolish when it comes to the legacy she planned to leave. I get a small settlement, but Charlotte and Picasso will receive most of it. The rest goes to some charitable foundation Bathsheba wanted established in her name."

"You didn't kill Bathsheba for her money?"

Liam took several steps back, his hand going to his chest. "Kill her? Of course not. It was a robbery gone wrong. The angels are just tying up the loose ends."

"You're absolutely sure that's what happened?" I asked.

"Well, yes. I mean, I have to assume that's what happened." He scratched his forehead. "As you know, it was dark inside the hospitality suite when the robbers entered. Do you think Bathsheba was killed by someone else?"

"You know Fanny well," I said, ignoring his question. "So you know about the rivalry between her and Bathsheba."

"Of course. It wasn't always pleasant to be around. Sometimes, they would have screeching rows that could be heard by everyone. It was embarrassing."

"Would Fanny have had an opportunity to come into the tent and attack Bathsheba the night of the concert?"

He blinked rapidly. "I.... well, I don't know about that. She's been inside the hospitality suite several times. She'd know the layout. It would have been easy for her to get in without anyone noticing. Are you really suggesting—"

"Their dislike of each other was genuine? Not some staged performance to grab headlines and keep their names in the limelight?"

"Of course, it was genuine. They've even had physical fights in the past and often sabotaged each other's performances. Once, Bathsheba put a magic laced drink in Fanny's dressing room. When it came to Fanny's time to perform, her voice had vanished. She wasn't able to sing for three weeks."

"That could have ruined Fanny's career." There goes another tick in the box for Fanny being involved in Bathsheba's murder.

"Which was exactly what Bathsheba wanted. She had an evil streak. She didn't care what she had to do so long as she stopped a rival from getting one over on her. Fanny's probably the best opera singer around. Bathsheba knew that. She despised Fanny because she could see she was about to be ousted from her throne."

The more I learned about Fanny, the more I became convinced that she'd killed Bathsheba. "When was the last time you saw Fanny before Bathsheba was killed?"

He shook his head. "No! I see where you're going with this, but Fanny isn't a murderer. She's a passionate woman but not a killer."

"I'm not so sure about that," I said. If I shared my theory about Fanny with Liam, he might open up or even slip up and tell me something useful that could put either of them in the frame. "I have my doubts that Mack and Coleman killed Bathsheba. They definitely stole from her, but someone else was involved in the murder. Think carefully. Did you see Fanny around the tent just before Bathsheba died?"

"She was definitely there. She came in to get her payment, and, well, in typical Bathsheba style, she decided not to give Fanny her earnings."

I nodded. "Fanny told me about that. She wasn't happy."

"Fanny was spitting mad. In fact... now I think about it, she threatened Bathsheba. She said that she wouldn't get away with it."

"What did Bathsheba do?"

"Laughed in her face and told her to go away. I was concerned about Fanny, but there was nothing I could do to help her. Bathsheba had full control over our finances. She didn't trust anyone when it came to money."

"After Fanny confronted Bathsheba, where did she go?"

"I'm not sure. She stomped out of the hospitality suite. It was late, so I assumed she went to the hotel."

"I don't think she did. Fanny stuck around," I said. "I don't know for sure, but maybe she even spotted Mack and Coleman creeping into the tent. When she realized they were robbing Bathsheba, she saw her opportunity to strike. You say that Fanny's a passionate woman. Maybe that passion spilled into a desire for revenge."

Liam groaned. "Don't say that I've made another terrible decision when it comes to women."

I patted him on the arm. "Maybe you have. Not only did you marry a tyrant, it looks like you might have been cheating on her with a murderer."

He sighed and shook his head. "It's just my luck. If only I had the willpower to remain celibate. Life would be so much easier."

"I don't doubt it." I suppressed a smirk. "How are Charlotte and Picasso doing?"

"They're very withdrawn. I don't know how to handle them. I've never taken to the role of stepdad. They don't take me seriously. I can't say I blame them. Should I mention your concerns about Fanny to them? Are we in any danger?"

"Don't say anything to Charlotte and Picasso. I don't think Fanny is interested in hurting any of you. This was all about getting even with Bathsheba. I need to speak to the angels, then we'll bring Fanny in for questioning. Keep this between us for now. I get that you like Fanny, but don't say anything to her."

"Oh! Of course not. I'm staying clear of her. I've had my fill of dangerous, overbearing women. Maybe it's time I tried the single life." He rubbed his chin. "Although being this handsome, there's so much temptation."

"You have my deepest sympathy. You should try the single life. It's not all that bad," I said. "You take care of Charlotte and Picasso. I've got someone I need to talk to."

I turned and spotted Wiggles flat out on the ground a dozen paces behind me. I hurried over. "What are you doing?"

"I collapsed with hunger about an hour ago. You didn't even notice."

"I'm noticing now. Move your behind."

"Are we finally getting pancakes?" He rolled onto his back and kicked his legs.

"Soon, I promise."

He growled. "Carry me."

"No! The exercise will do you good. Come on. We need to see the angels."

I walked toward the village then glanced back over my shoulder. Wiggles hadn't moved. "Get up!"

"Pancakes!"

"We have a murder to solve."

"I can't think without fuel inside me."

"You're not helping. I'll leave you here. The stone circle might notice you if you're not careful."

"Do you think it will feed me pancakes?"

"No, it will fry your fuzzy butt for being so lazy." With a sigh, I hurried back, scooped him into my arms, and strode away.

He licked my cheek. "Pancakes?"

"I'll pancake you if you keep fooling around. We have to convince the angels that Fanny was involved with this murder."

"And if we can't?"

"Then I'll bring her down and get the confession for myself. No one commits murder in my village and gets away with it."

Chapter 12

A short walk through the village with Wiggles still in my arms found me standing outside Angel Force. The usually pristine white walls were covered in smears of dirt, and graffiti covered one wall.

Three angels almost slammed into me as they hurried through the doors.

"Where's the fire?" I spotted Dominic among them.

"Over in the forest," he said.

"I was joking." I took a step closer to him. "There's really a fire?"

"It's only small, but we need to put it out before it gets out of hand."

"Make sure Fallon knows," I said. "She'll help you out."

He waved as he raced after his colleagues, and the three of them took to the sky on their giant white wings.

I entered the reception lobby and discovered it buzzing with activity.

Dazielle stood behind the desk, a line of concentration between her eyebrows. The stern expression on her face only deepened when she spotted me. "What are you doing here?"

"I'm here to convince you that Mack and Coleman are innocent."

"I know. Well, they're innocent of murder."

"You finally agree with me that they didn't kill Bathsheba?" This could be easier than I'd anticipated.

Dazielle's tongue poked out from between her teeth before she nodded. "I do."

"Can I speak to them and see if they have useful information about the actual killer?"

"Not a chance," Dazielle said. "They're not getting out of here. I haven't made the charges formal yet, but they had the jewels on them and have been identified by the family as the individuals who stole from the tent. They'll serve time for what they did."

"What made you change your mind about them?"

Dazielle huffed out a breath. "I bet you're loving this."

"Maybe just a tiny bit." I tried not to smile too broadly. "I did suggest that they weren't powerful enough to have killed Bathsheba after I'd caught them."

"With my help," Wiggles said.

"Of course, always with your help. We couldn't have done it without you," I said.

"I'm sure we would have managed without either of you interfering," Dazielle said.

"Go on. What changed your mind?" I set Wiggles down on the floor.

Dazielle checked some paperwork and handed it to a passing angel. "I had their magic tested. Neither of them was powerful enough to produce a lethal magic bolt spell."

"Which is something I may have mentioned." This time, I allowed the smugness to seep through.

"Yes, you're the clever one." Dazielle's wings fluttered around her.

"So, what's next?"

"In reference to..."

"In reference to you finding the actual killer? I've got a few ideas if you want to hear them."

"I really don't," Dazielle said. "Mack and Coleman are talking, and we're getting useful information. Initially, they panicked and pointed the finger at each other. Mack said that Coleman fired the spell, and he said the exact same thing about Mack."

"So, you thought you had the case wrapped up?"

She nodded. "I figured it was only a matter of time before one of them broke, but it didn't happen. After we tested them, we realized neither of them could have cast that spell. They both lied. It was after that that they admitted somebody paid them to rob Bathsheba."

I leaned closer. "Who paid them?"

"They don't know. They received a message telling them where Bathsheba would be and what jewelry she'd have on her. It was too much of a temptation. Not only were they getting paid for this job, they'd also get away with a sack load of jewels they could pawn."

"They were set up." I slapped my hand on the counter. "The killer used them as a distraction, so she could sneak in and kill Bathsheba during the chaos of the robbery."

"It sounds like you know who did it." Dazielle jerked her chin up. "Reveal your stunning revelation."

"It was Fanny. I'm certain of it. Bathsheba cheated her out of her earnings from the performance. They'd been bitter rivals for years. Whenever they performed together, they'd sabotage each other. Fanny's hatred ran deep. And to top it all, she has her eye on Liam. And he's interested in her too. I discovered him slipping away from Fanny's hotel room this morning. He admitted he was unhappy with Bathsheba and planned to move on. Straight into Fanny's waiting bed."

Dazielle ran a hand down one wing. "We should speak to Fanny about this."

"We?"

"Don't get too smug," she said. "Since you figured this out, you may as well come along while I make the arrest. And all my angels are busy fighting other fires."

"Literally from the sounds of things. I saw Dominic heading off to put out a blaze in the forest."

Dazielle blew out a breath. Dark undereye circles marred her usually perfect face. "That's just one of a dozen reports that have already come in this morning. It's a case of all hands on deck. Even if those hands are yours."

I chose to ignore that insult. "Sounds good to me. When do you want to bring Fanny in?"

"Now is good. If I don't get out of here soon, my head will explode. Everyone wants a piece of me, and there's only so much to go around."

"It's a hard life being the boss."

Dazielle grunted. "Don't I know it. Let's move."

I winked at Wiggles. "We're back on the team."

"Does that mean I can go in the office?" Wiggles shuffled toward the closing door that led to the angels' desks, the cells, and most importantly for him, food.

"No!" Dazielle yanked open the front door. "You're both with me."

"You can grab the stale doughnuts another day." I blocked Wiggles' attempt to get through the door and tried to steer him outside.

His eyes glowed red. He looked like he was about to act up again. "I won't forget this. There's food in there calling my name."

"I'm not asking you to. But we need to speak with Fanny."

He sat and glared at me.

I raised my hands in defeat. "You're a troublemaker." I strode into the back room and spotted a pile of pink iced doughnuts sitting on a table. I grabbed one and raced out, shoving it straight in Wiggles' mouth.

"No more misbehaving, or I'm leaving you back home."

He wagged his tail as he trotted happily along beside me. "When do I ever misbehave?"

I gave him the stink eye before we chased after Dazielle.

"I'll ask the questions." She strode ahead of us, heading in the direction of the hotel. "You can be the muscle."

"May I ask one question?"

"No."

"Two questions?"

Dazielle grunted again.

I lifted a hand. "Got it. I'll stand there and look menacing and make sure Fanny doesn't make a run for it. Even though you're eight inches taller than me and have those enormous wings that expand six feet on either side of you, I'll be much better at ensuring the suspect doesn't escape."

Dazielle slid me a glance but didn't say anything.

"Am I forgiven yet over the whole Isaac Dubrov debacle?"

"No."

That was reassuring. "Any word on how Oriel's doing?"

"Still unconscious. And still waiting for her fruit basket from you. You haven't been to see her yet."

"I haven't forgotten," I said. "But I was thinking, if she's unconscious, she won't want fruit. Maybe I could get her something to play music on. Don't unconscious people still hear things going on around them?"

"So the doctor claims," Dazielle said. "He recommends we talk to Oriel when we visit."

"I'll do that then. Music is better than fruit."

"Nothing too violent," Dazielle said.

"Violent? Music isn't violent."

"I'm referring to your metal nights at Cloven Hoof. You like music sung by growly men with noisy guitars."

"Rock at its finest," I said. "I make no apologies for that."

"Get Oriel something soothing to listen to. Nothing that agitates."

"If I play her rock music, and she hates it, she might wake up to ask me to turn down the volume."

That earned me another angry grunt.

We reached the hotel and walked into the lobby.

Tabitha sat behind the desk, her eyes widening when she saw us. "This looks official. I'm assuming you don't want a room."

"Not today. This is very official," I said. "Angel business."

"Why are you here if that's the case?" Tabitha asked.

"I'm a temporary angel," I said.

"That's never going to happen," Dazielle said. "Tabitha, we're here to see Fanny Flotella. Which room is she in?"

"Number six, top of the stairs on the right. I don't want any trouble, though," Tabitha said.

"When do the angels ever cause you trouble?" I said.

"I'm not worried about Dazielle. I don't want any of my walls singed, Tempest Crypt. Trouble is never far behind you."

"I'll be on my best behavior." I fluttered my lashes.

"Humph," Tabitha said. "And I know what your dog is like when he gets gassy and excited."

"Hey! Anyone can have an accident." Wiggles lifted his nose in the air and walked away.

We headed up the stairs, and Dazielle knocked on the bedroom door.

When Fanny pulled it open, she jerked back. "I wasn't expecting company. I'm busy right now."

"This will only take a few moments," Dazielle said. "We have questions regarding Bathsheba's murder."

She shook her head. "I have nothing more to say. I really must get on."

"And you'll be able to do that once we've asked our questions." I pushed past Dazielle and edged into the room.

Fanny followed me, her hands clasped together. There was an open suitcase on her bed that was half full.

"Going somewhere?" I asked.

"Of course. There's nothing left for me here. I'm not getting paid for my performance, so I need to go earn money elsewhere." Fanny flung some clothes into the case.

This looked like the actions of a guilty woman. She was planning on fleeing the crime scene. Maybe Liam had tipped her off, despite me asking him to keep quiet.

"You'll need to stay around a while longer," Dazielle said. "The men we initially thought murdered Bathsheba are innocent."

Fanny stopped folding a long purple dress into her case and stared at Dazielle. "That's not possible. They killed her. Everyone saw what happened."

"The problem is, they didn't," I said. "The killer used a darkness spell. Although people could hear things going on, nobody actually saw who fired the fatal blow that killed Bathsheba."

"I don't know anything about that." Fanny stuffed the dress into her case. "Bathsheba has caused me nothing but trouble. I'm not going to pretend I'm sad about what happened. At least now I can move on with my life without looking over my shoulder and worrying that she's coming for me."

"I'd like you to go over your movements again on the night of Bathsheba's murder," Dazielle said.

"Why? I didn't kill her."

"It'll help us clear up the timeline," Dazielle said. "You finished your performance, and then what happened?"

"I've already gone over this."

"One more time," Dazielle said, "just in case I missed something relevant."

Fanny blew out a breath. "I did the warmup act, then Bathsheba performed. I left her alone for a while once the concert ended. She always got highly strung after singing. It often led to an argument if she was approached too soon. Then I went into the tent to get my money. Bathsheba refused to give me my cut. I was so angry. Nobody stepped in to help. I was on my own. Before I said something I'd regret, I left, walked around to calm down, and came back here." She jabbed a finger at me. "You found me here."

"But you hadn't been here long," I said. "Tabitha said you only got back ten minutes before I arrived."

"And you've openly admitted to hating Bathsheba," Dazielle said.

"Nearly everybody who worked with Bathsheba hated her. She was a hard woman to love. She let her talent go to her head. If anything, I pitied her. She was surrounded by people who lied to her face about how incredible she was and how much they adored her then gossiped about her behind her back. Who'd want to live a life like that?"

"What about your relationship with Liam?" I asked.

That earned me an angry tut from Dazielle, but I was determined to get my questions in.

"What about it?" Fanny tilted her head, her eyes shining.

"I saw him leave the hotel this morning, and you followed him," I said. "He admitted to having a relationship with you."

She waved a hand in the air. "He may call it a relationship. I simply call it passing the time."

"You're not in love with Liam?" I asked.

"I mean, I might lust after Liam. He's a gorgeous guy. He should be on the covers of magazines wearing nothing but a tiny pair of bathing trunks and an alluring smile. The man looks like he was created in the image of some angelic creature. You just want to eat him up."

"He seems sweet on you," I said.

A smile softened her face. "Liam's a cutie pie. I have fun with him. But I'm not after anything serious. He's stunning, but he's dumb. And it did feel great to get one over on Bathsheba by getting him in my bed after months of frustrating flirting."

"You were seeing Liam behind Bathsheba's back?" I asked.

"Nothing happened other than a few stolen kisses whilst Bathsheba was still alive," Fanny said. "But Liam was soon knocking at my door once she was gone. He said he'd never felt so free and wanted to celebrate. And boy, can that man celebrate."

I hid a smile behind my hand as I scrubbed my cheek. "Lucky you. You have no plans to make the relationship official?"

"Of course not. I won't mind hanging out with him again a few times, but I'll be busy now Bathsheba's gone. There'll be plenty of events that have lost their famous opera singer and are looking for someone to step in and replace her. By the end of the week, I could be on the other side of the world performing to an adoring crowd."

"Not if you killed Bathsheba," Dazielle said.

Fanny dropped the last of her clothes into the case. "I'm innocent. I understand why you might think otherwise, but it wasn't me. If it's any help, I saw those two guys lurking around near the tent when I left. I didn't pay them much attention because I was in such a terrible mood, but they looked suspicious. They had a dangerous air about them. Maybe if I hadn't been so angry, I may have realized that they were up to something dodgy."

I shook my head. Fanny was trying to deflect attention from herself by pointing the finger back at Mack and Coleman. She had the motive and the opportunity, but did she have the power to kill?

"Do you know how to perform a magic bolt spell?" It was as if Dazielle had read my mind.

"I know of the spell, of course, but I've never used it," Fanny said.

"So you won't mind showcasing your magic for us now," Dazielle said. "If only to exclude you from our ongoing investigation."

"I don't have the time," Fanny said. "I plan to leave this afternoon. I still have my packing to finish."

"Five minutes won't be a problem," I said. "Show us your magic."

Fanny rubbed the end of her nose. "This is most inconvenient."

"A quick spell. That's all we want to see," I said. "Once we're done, Dazielle will arrange for first class travel to wherever you wish to go."

"I will?"

I nudged her. "Of course. Fanny is helping us, and we want to make life easy on her."

Dazielle scowled at me. "I'll consider it."

Fanny sighed. "Oh, very well, providing you stop bothering me." She twisted her wrists and flipped her hands. A shower of sparkles drifted in the air.

"Is that it?" I asked.

"I've never been a strong magic user. I've always honed my singing rather than my magic. It's what I'm known for. Why use magic when you have something as pure as my voice?"

"Try again." I wasn't convinced that was the best Fanny had.

She shrugged and shook her head. "That's it."

"I don't believe you." I shot a light ball over her head.

Fanny yelped and ducked.

"Tempest! That's not necessary," Dazielle said. "Fanny has shown us her ability."

"She's only shown us a fraction of what she can do," I said. "Come on. You need to defend yourself. Show us what you're made of." The next blast of my magic skimmed the top of her head.

Fanny flung herself on the bed. "Stop her! She's trying to kill me." Her wide eyes fixed onto Dazielle.

"What about this?" I shot another spell at her.

Fanny squeaked and dodged the spell, rolling over and clutching a pillow to her face.

I threw two more blasts of magic at her.

"Stop doing that! Make her stop! Dazielle, you're supposed to uphold the law in this village. Surely it's illegal to try to kill a person." Fanny flipped off the bed and ducked by the side, just the top of her head showing.

"That's quite enough, Tempest," Dazielle said. "If Fanny could fight back, she would. Perhaps you should apologize."

"You're right. I feel terrible." I walked around the side of the bed and held out my hand. "I didn't mean to go that far. Will you accept my apology?"

"I guess so." Fanny sniffed and went to grab my hand.

I shot a stinging blast of magic straight at her. It punched into her chest, and she slammed into the floor.

With a squeal of rage, Fanny launched herself at me, her hands outstretched. Angry sparks of jagged magic flashed from her fingers and blasted the wall just above my head.

"That's it." I grinned as I dodged her magic onslaught. "I knew your true power was hiding somewhere."

"You could have killed me!" She tried to hit me with more magic. "You've singed the ends of my hair. I hate having my hair cut."

The room crackled with her power, and the whites of her eyes glowed. Oh yes, Fanny Flotella was more than your average magic user.

"Have you seen enough?" I hit the floor as Fanny blasted another spell at me.

Dazielle was tight-lipped as she nodded.

"Then arrest her!" I yelled.

Dazielle flew in the air, her wings extended, before she descended on Fanny and wrapped them around her. "Fanny Flotella, I'm arresting you on suspicion of Bathsheba Delaware's murder."

Muffled protests came from inside the wings as Fanny squirmed and fought against the power of Dazielle's wings.

I sighed as I rolled onto my back. Wiggles jumped on my chest and licked my cheek. "Congratulations. We caught the killer."

"We did." I nodded as I lifted him off my chest and sat up, leaning my back against the wall.

"Let's hope we got the right person this time," Dazielle said. "Have you been to see the stone circle since the evening of the concert?"

"I was about to take a look when I saw Liam this morning and got distracted," I said. "What are they doing?"

"You should see for yourself but make sure you take your hardhat. Those stones are still unhappy."

I stood and placed Wiggles on the floor. "Not for much longer. This case has been solved. Although I've yet to hear a word of thanks from you."

"And payment. I take doughnuts. Any flavor," Wiggles said.

Dazielle flipped her hair back. "Consider the fact I'm not arresting you for what happened to our evidence store thanks enough."

I shrugged. "I'll take it." I'd also take some sweet treats. Solving a murder made me hungry.

Chapter 13

"How many times do I have to tell you it wasn't me?" A protesting Fanny was led out of the hotel by Dazielle.

"Can you handle things from here?" I asked her.

"I don't know how I ever managed without you, Tempest." Dazielle shook her head.

"That's good to know. I'm going to take a look at the stone circle while I'm here."

"Have fun," Dazielle said before she turned Fanny and led her away.

I blew out a breath, a deep sense of satisfaction settling over me. The murder had been solved. The real killer was finally in custody, and I could relax.

"So, time to celebrate?" Wiggles said.

"Almost. Let's take a peek at the stone circle. Then I'll treat us both to something delicious."

"Brownies," Wiggles said. "No, pink iced doughnuts. Or pancakes. I can take a stack of pancakes any time of the day. Maybe a cream horn. Or—"

"Stop! You're making me drool."

Wiggles continued to shout out dessert names as we climbed the hill to the stone circle. The good mood I'd been feeling faded as I came face-to-face with a crackling mass of dark energy that sat over the top of the stones.

I slowed, my mouth falling open. "What's been going on here?"

"Huh! Maybe the stone circle doesn't know that Fanny's been arrested," Wiggles said.

"Or they don't care," I said. "I've never felt them emit energy like this before. It feels... broken."

"Blood has been spilled on their territory," Wiggles said. "That's gonna make them tetchy."

I edged closer to the stone circle. The ground beneath my feet vibrated, rattling my teeth.

"Maybe you shouldn't get any nearer," Wiggles said. "I don't like the way the ground is pulsing."

"It feels like the stone circle's heartbeat. And it's way too fast." A rapid thud-thud-thud pounded beneath us, shaking soil loose from around the base of the stones. "It reminds me of a volcano that's about to blow."

"Have you ever been around when a volcano's gone boom?" Wiggles asked.

"No! But it's that tension in the air, like everything's on a knife's edge and about to slide the wrong way."

"Let's go get that cake now. If this is my last day as a hellhound, I want to be eating cake when I go."

"Let's just see if we can calm things down here." I looked around the stones and cleared my throat. "You can relax now. Everything's under control. We've discovered who killed Bathsheba. Fanny will be charged any time now. Justice will be served."

The rumbling under my feet increased.

"That didn't work," Wiggles said. "We should offer the stones something to eat."

"What are you thinking, human or animal sacrifice?"

"I was actually thinking about pizza," Wiggles said.

I took another step toward the stones. They crackled with red energy, and a tornado spun around the inside of the circle. The stones were doing their utmost to keep people away.

"Listen, how about—" I was flung from my feet as a blast of the stones' red magic punched into my chest. I smashed to the ground, my ears ringing and my vision blurry.

"Are you okay?" Wiggles' face appeared over mine, and he sniffed my nose.

"Not really." I tested my fingers and toes. Everything worked.

"I did tell you not to get any closer," Wiggles said. "You don't have to be a genius to figure out the stone circle is seriously cheesed off about something."

"Yeah, I just about managed to work that out." After checking to make sure no bones were broken, I eased myself into a seated position.

I glanced at Wiggles and snorted a laugh of pure surprise. "You're purple!"

"I'm what now?" He flipped his head from side to side. "Hey! Look at that. And it's more puce than purple."

"Did the stones get you too?" I asked.

"I got a little zap in the behind when I was running after you," he said. "If you think this is bad, you should see your hair."

"My... hair?" I grabbed a handful of hair and pulled it in front of my face. It was pink and sparkling. "Are you kidding me?"

Wiggles snorted a laugh. "It's cute. You look like a giant candy floss. I might even lick you."

"Keep your licks to yourself," I said. "Hey, stones, change my hair color back."

The ground rumbled. That sounded like a definite no.

I sighed as I climbed to my feet and brushed the dust off the back of my pants. "Maybe it's just a matter of time. Once the angels charge Fanny, the stones will relax and go back to their normal chilled out state."

"And if they don't?" Wiggles sniffed his purple fur.

"Then it's time we consider moving somewhere new. I don't want to live in a village where magic is out of control and the only color my hair can be is sparkly pink."

"You'd never leave Willow Tree Falls."

"You don't mind being a purple hellhound?"

"Nope. And I'm a puce hellhound."

"That sounds so much worse."

"I'll need a new batch of bow ties if I'm staying this color. My red ones will clash with the puce."

I shook my head. "That's really all you're worried about?"

He cocked his head. "It's not the only thing. How about we go check on Bandit?"

"You mean your best friend?" I grinned at him.

Wiggles snorted. "I know she's fooling everyone with her pretend illness. I want to catch her out and figure out how she's doing it. Then I can use it to fake my own illness and make people run around after me and give into my every whim."

"Sure you do. Okay, why not? I want to check in on Aurora's store and make sure everything's behaving itself. And she always has food."

I kept examining my hair as we walked back to the village. Pink didn't suit me. I was a black kind of girl. I always had been. I knew black. I liked it. I'd never been into pink, even when I was a child.

I walked into Heaven's Door with Wiggles. Aurora stood behind the counter, wrapping a package.

She grinned when she saw me. "Hurrah! Your hair's a funky color too."

"I'd rather have green than pink." I slid onto a stool beside the counter. "The stone circle told me exactly what it thought of my suggestion to calm down."

"I heard the stones are still misbehaving," Aurora said. "Maybe you shouldn't have gotten so close."

"That's exactly what I told her," Wiggles said.

"How's Bandit doing today?" I looked around for any sign of Bandit's favorite cardboard box, but it was nowhere to be seen.

"She's in my apartment," Aurora said. "And she's not doing so well. She did eat a bit more but then got tired. I thought a rest would do her good. I didn't want the customers bothering her, so I moved her out of the way."

"Good thinking. She might bite them if she's still in a bad mood."

"She tried that twice with me before I got her settled."

"Never trust a cat," Wiggles said. "The second they lull you into a false sense of safety, they go for you. It happens all the time."

Aurora dabbed at a row of fresh scratches on her hand. "I'm beginning to realize that."

"We've solved the murder," I said. "If the stone circle is making Bandit ill, she should start to feel better soon."

"That's great news. Who killed Bathsheba?" Aurora asked.

"It was Fanny."

"You thought it might be her," Aurora said. "She's confessed?"

"Not exactly, but she will. I convinced Dazielle that she needs to be the prime suspect. Everything points to her."

"Dazielle must have been desperate for help," Aurora said. "She rarely listens to you."

"Thanks for that ringing endorsement."

Aurora chuckled. "What's going to happen to Bathsheba's children?"

"They're old enough to look after themselves," I said. "And now they're also stinking rich. They can do what they like."

"That's a good motive for murder." Aurora arched an eyebrow. "I'm just saying, with Bathsheba dead, the children will inherit a lot of money."

"I'm sure Fanny's behind this. Dazielle can tie up the loose ends and get her to confess."

"How kind of you to let her finish doing her job." Aurora laughed and shook her head.

"That's me. Generous to a fault. How about you show us what you've got in your cake tin, then we'll do some more magic on Bandit? It might be just the extra nudge she needs to recover."

"Perfect idea," Aurora said. "Although I'm all out of cake."

Wiggles staggered to the side, and his tail drooped. "Did I hear you right? You always have cake."

"Not today. I've been too busy looking after Bandit and keeping the store calm. The cake tin is bare."

"This is a national disaster." Wiggles turned to the door. "I must have cake."

"I may get a chance to bake something later," Aurora said. "Tempest, you finish tying up this package. Make sure you do the bows neatly and double knot it. We don't want anything falling out when it's delivered. I'll go grab Bandit from upstairs."

I stared at the package. I couldn't tie a neat bow to save my life. I had a few attempts and abandoned it. Aurora would only complain if I didn't do it properly.

She appeared in the doorway, carrying Bandit in her cardboard box, swaddled in blankets. She was panting.

Wiggles sniffed loudly as he approached the counter. "She still stinks."

"She does smell a bit pungent," Aurora said. "It's not as bad as when she was in your apartment. That's a good sign."

I cracked my knuckles and rolled my wrists. "Let's do this."

We spent the next few minutes running spells over Bandit. They attached easily, and it wasn't long before she was blinking and yawning.

She arched her back and stretched before turning in her box. Her gaze latched onto me. "Tempest!"

"That's me," I said. "How are you feeling?"

"Don't worry about me. I remember everything!" Bandit said.

"Which is what?"

"The message. What I was supposed to tell you. Your dad. He's alive!" She staggered to the side, groaned, and collapsed into her box.

I stared first at Bandit and then Aurora, my heart thumping out a rapid rhythm. "What just happened?"

"I... don't know." Aurora ran her hands over Bandit. "Oh! She's burning up again. She was getting better. She responded so well to our magic."

I peered at the panting cat. "Bandit mentioned our dad. Why?"

"It's probably her fever making her talk nonsense," Aurora said. "I've mentioned him to her. She knows that I'm worried about him. Maybe it's on Bandit's mind."

I pressed either side of my temple with my fingers. "I guess. She can't know anything about him though, can she? She said she had a message for me."

"How would Bandit know anything about him?" Aurora kept a hand on Bandit's stomach.

"She shouldn't." Uneasiness stirred through me. Something felt wrong here, and it wasn't just the hinky magic vibe the stone circle was kicking out.

"Maybe we should try to wake Bandit," I said. "She could remember more of the message. She might have useful information about Dad."

Aurora shook her head. "We can't risk it. She was just talking nonsense. Pay no attention to her. People say strange things when they have a fever."

I bit my bottom lip as I slid from the stool and stepped away. Something felt really wrong here. What did Bandit know about our dad? Was she involved with his disappearance? Did she know something about it? Had she caused it to happen?

Bandit had to get better. This could be the missing piece in the puzzle to locate Dad. I had to find out what the rest of her message was.

Chapter 14

After spending a couple of hours with Aurora in the store, trying to bring down Bandit's fever without much success, I headed back to Cloven Hoof with Wiggles.

We went to grab a box of apple turnovers and maple pecan brownies from Sprinkles, but the place was still closed. If we wanted cake, I'd have to make it for us, and I wasn't quite that desperate.

Instead of risking a baking disaster, I discovered a half-eaten cherry cake in the fridge in the club kitchen, which ended up perched on my desk, a large slice cut off for Wiggles.

I put my head down and got to work, but the whole time I was checking through paperwork, my mind churned over what Bandit had said. She had information she needed to tell me.

She'd said Dad was alive. Although Aurora thought it was a coincidence, I wasn't so sure. The way Bandit had suddenly turned up in the village was unusual, as was the magic that had turned her into a cat.

I needed to get Bandit well before I could find out more.

Aurora, quite rightly, had refused to push too hard with the magic to get Bandit talking again. She didn't want her getting worse.

And I got that, but I hated having to wait.

Granny Dottie hurried through the doorway of my office. "Why didn't you tell me that my marvelous birthday gift had been murdered?"

"Um... I've been a bit busy. How come you're only just hearing about it?"

She brushed her wild hair off her face and cut herself a piece of cake. "We've been busy at the demon prison. You'd know that if you bothered to stop by."

My eyebrows shot up. "The demons are acting up?"

"I should say they are." She bit into the cake. "This would go down well with a lemon drop."

I pushed my seat back and stood. "I've had enough of paperwork. I'll take the cake. You lead the way."

We walked into the quiet bar, just a few members of staff in there setting up for the evening.

I set the cake down and poured two lemon drops.

Granny downed hers and tapped the empty glass for another one.

I caught hold of her chin and twisted her face to the side. "What's with all the bruises?" My gaze went to her cut knuckles. "Have you been in a fight?"

"It's the demons. I've been smacking them down for hours."

I blew out a breath. "I had no idea things were so bad at the prison. Although the whole village has been playing up. I should have assumed the demons would get a sense that things were out of kilter and push their luck. Do you need an extra pair of hands?"

She dismissed my comment with a wave. "Of course not. We can handle a few angry demons. But they are proving tricky. I got caught unawares."

"Were you napping again?"

"The cheek! I never nap when on duty. I simply close my eyes when I'm having serious thoughts that require my full attention."

"Have you been having a lot of serious thoughts lately?" I refilled her glass.

"That's enough sass from you." Granny Dottie took a sip. "So, who killed my birthday gift?"

"The warmup act, Fanny Flotella," I said. "The angels took her into custody today."

"That charming woman." Granny Dottie shook her head. "I'd never have thought it. She sang like an angel."

"She's a devil in disguise," I said. "There were serious issues between her and Bathsheba. Plus, Fanny was having naughty fun with Liam, the husband, behind Bathsheba's back."

Granny Dottie tutted. "Well, I can understand that. That man is certainly easy on the eye."

"Just like Grandpa Lucius, don't you think?" Granny was an outrageous flirt but was devoted to my grandpa.

"He'll always be my one and only love, but it doesn't hurt to admire a beautiful form now and again." She grabbed my hand. "What about

Bathsheba's poor children? I know she adopted two from an article I read about her."

"Children who are grown adults and about to become ridiculously rich. I think they'll figure things out just fine."

"I saw the boy outside," Granny Dottie said. "When they were younger, Bathsheba would take them on her tours and have pictures with them all in their best outfits. It was sweet. He hasn't changed much. He never smiled in those pictures. He looks like a sullen young man."

"You mean Picasso?"

She nodded. "It looked like he was waiting for someone. Maybe he's coming in here. You can ask him all about his inheritance."

My gaze lifted to the door as Merrie unlocked it. I'd been meaning to speak to Charlotte and Picasso when they weren't with Liam. There didn't seem much point now that Fanny was on the hook for Bathsheba's murder.

"And if things don't work out between you and Rhett, you could always grab yourself a rich toy boy," Granny Dottie said.

I snorted a laugh. "I'll pass on that idea. Sullen young men don't interest me. Besides, I'm happy with Rhett."

"Rhett may not be rich, but he sure is handsome. You hang on to that one."

"I plan to."

Picasso Delaware walked through the doorway of the club. He was dressed head to toe in black, his dreadlocks tied off his face.

"Speak of the devil," I said. "You were right."

"I always am," Granny Dottie said.

"Have another drink." I gave her a double lemon shot before I slid around the bar and headed to the booth Picasso had settled in.

His dark gaze shifted to me before he looked away.

"What will it be?" I asked.

"I didn't know you worked here."

"I own the place."

"Do you do White Russians?" His gaze flicked to me.

"Sure, we do. We do all the cocktails. Magical or non-magical?"

"I don't care," he said. "And some of those dried mushrooms I keep hearing about in the village. They're supposed to be good."

"They're the best. Any particular blend?"

"Whatever you think is best." He sighed and looked away.

"You must be having a tough time with everything that's going on," I said.

He lifted one shoulder.

"How's your sister doing?" I asked.

"She'll be here soon, so you can ask her yourself."

"Did you hear the angels arrested Fanny for your mom's murder?"

"I did. Honestly, so long as they catch whoever did it, I don't care. They just need to be put away for a long time. I want this finished."

"Have the police been over what happened with you that night?"

"Only about a dozen times," he said.

"And did you see Fanny in the tent?"

"Of course not. It was dark. All I'm thankful for is that my sister wasn't killed."

"It's good that you look out for her. You seem close."

"We grew up together."

He was a chatty one. "And how's your arm injury?"

"It's fine." He rubbed the place where he'd been injured.

"Can you think of a reason the robbers struck out at you as well?"

"I can guess. Maybe a magic blast backfired, or they were worried I might fight back, so they wanted to disable me." His gaze lifted to the door. "Now if you don't mind, there's my sister. We'd appreciate some privacy."

I nodded at Charlotte as she arrived at the booth and slid in opposite Picasso.

"She'll have the same as me," he said.

"I expect now your mom's murder is solved, you'll be leaving," I said.

Picasso simply glowered. It didn't bother me. I wasn't here to make friends.

Charlotte glanced at him before nodding. "That's right. The angels have everything they need. I'll be glad to get out of here. We need time to mourn. It's a difficult thing to do when your mom was such a public figure. We've been hounded by people asking for quotes they can use and pictures of us. Someone even suggested I send them a picture of the body. It makes me sick. Why can't everybody leave us alone?"

"That's just what I was telling Tempest. We need our privacy." Picasso twisted his left shoulder, turning his back to me.

I took that as my cue to leave and headed to the bar with their order. For grieving children, they didn't seem that devastated about losing their mom. I'd be in pieces if my mom ever got sick, let alone anything worse.

Although if Bathsheba had been hard on them just like she'd been with Liam and Fanny, maybe they had no reason to be sad. They might even be secretly relieved about what happened but didn't want to show it.

With my thoughts still focused on Bandit's mysterious comments, I worked on auto pilot for the rest of the evening and barely had time to think about Fanny, Bathsheba, or anything else. That case was closed.

I crashed into bed just after three in the morning and went off into a deep sleep, confident that order had been restored in Willow Tree Falls once again.

***

"They must have drunk so much as a way of coping." Wiggles snuffled around the trash can as I finished the last of my cereal and coffee the next morning.

"Charlotte and Picasso were definitely tipsy last night when they left the club," I said. "Maybe you're right. People handle grief in different ways."

"I'd definitely be eating lots if I was sad," Wiggles said.

"No surprise there," I said. "You eat for any reason. You might be happy, sad, angry, bored."

"I'm an emotional eater." He lifted his head. "Speaking of eating—"

"You just had breakfast!"

"Not food for me. We should get brownies for Bandit," he said. "They might make her feel better."

"I knew you cared about her," I said.

"I never said that." He sniffed around for a few seconds. "She only eats food that's the color of nature. Brownies are bark colored."

"We can go get brownies if you like. There's always room for brownies."

"We can go to Sprinkles and see if it's open this time," Wiggles said. "Patti's brownies can't be beaten."

"Then Sprinkles it is."

Twenty minutes later, we were out of the apartment and walking along the unusually quiet street. It wasn't that early in the day; it was almost pushing noon, but there was barely anyone around. The clouds overhead were still a strange yellow, and the tense atmosphere flicking around me made me speed up as I headed to Patti's store.

A string of curses flew out the back room as we walked to the counter.

I ducked as a currant bun shot off the shelf and almost smacked me on the forehead.

Patti bustled out, a tray of burnt scones in her hand and her hair a disheveled mess around her head. "Oh! Tempest. I meant to put the lock on the door. I'm not open today. As you can see, things in the store aren't behaving themselves."

I batted another currant bun out of my way as it tried to whack my nose. "This must be the work of the stone circle. Is it still playing up? It should have calmed down by now."

"I haven't been over to see it, but it must be." She slammed the tray down. "I've wasted the whole morning trying to bake. Everything is either burnt or undercooked. The oven temperature won't stay constant, and just when I thought I'd gotten things figured out, it went wrong again. And I'm sure some of my ingredients have been mixed up. When I tried my first batch of sponge cakes this morning, they tasted of salt. I never mix up my ingredients. Everything is clearly labeled."

"I suppose it's too much to ask that you've got any edible brownies in stock?" I said. "Wiggles wants to get his best friend a gift."

"That's sweet," Patti said.

"She's not my best friend." Wiggles lifted his nose. "Are you going to throw those scones away?"

"Of course! They're a singed nightmare."

"I'll have them."

"We're here for brownies for Bandit," I said. "Leave the burnt scones alone."

"Oh! I heard she wasn't well. I saw Aurora a couple of days ago, and she mentioned how worried she was," Patti said. "The only thing I can offer you are frozen brownies. I can defrost them, but they're not as good as fresh."

"Whatever you've got will be fine," I said.

"Let's hope the microwave doesn't explode. Back in a moment." Patti hurried off to the back room, and I spent the next couple of minutes dodging flying cakes and avoiding getting a black eye from the flapjacks and cream horns that whizzed around.

Wiggles, on the other hand, was having a great time. He'd already caught three Belgian buns and a unicorn cookie in his mouth.

"Not bad," he said as he munched the cookie. "There are too many spices, though, and maybe some Tabasco sauce."

I stuck my tongue out. "Spit it out. That can't be good for you."

"It all ends up in the same place," Wiggles said. "Sweet and savory. I love both."

"Here we go. These should see you right." Patti returned and passed me a bag. "And on the house if they're for the sick patient."

"Thanks," I said.

"Oh! And can you ask Aurora to let me know when she's open for business again?" Patti said.

"She should be open today."

"That's what I thought. When I walked past Heaven's Door this morning, it was shut. She's always the first to open in the village. I figured she'd decided to batten down the hatches until the magic settles. That's what I plan to do if the oven refuses to cooperate."

My eyebrows rose. "That's odd. Maybe Bandit's not doing so well so Aurora's looking after her. I'll make sure she lets you know when she's open again. Thanks for these." I lifted the bag of brownies as I hurried out of Sprinkles.

Wiggles was way ahead of me, sprinting to Aurora's store.

Sure enough, when we got there, the blinds were down, and the door locked.

Wiggles placed his paws on the window ledge and peered through. "There's no one in there. All the lights are off."

I used an unlock spell and shoved the door open. A strange, swampy herb-like smell drifted out the door. Aurora's store always smelled of herbs, but this had an unhealthy whiff to it, a bit like a combination between a rancid bog and a blocked toilet.

"Hello?" I stepped inside the gloomy store, Wiggles right beside me.

"Where are they?" He shoved past me and lifted his nose. "Something smells terrible in here, and it's not that manky old cat."

I nodded as I crept farther into the store. The whole place had a seriously bad vibe to it. My nerves jangled. It felt like I was about to be stomped on by something huge, violent, and angry.

A quick search of the store revealed neither Aurora nor Bandit.

I hurried through the store and along the back corridor, climbing the steep steps to Aurora's apartment. I tried the handle, but it was locked.

Wiggles sniffed along the crack at the bottom of the door. "That weird smell is strongest in there. It's coming from her apartment."

I knocked and, for a second, detected shuffling on the other side before there was silence.

"Maybe Aurora's got Lex in there." Wiggles tilted his head. "We could be disturbing her fun times."

I pressed a hand against my nose, my stomach recoiling at the weird stench. I couldn't wait any longer. I had to find out what was happening on the other side of the door.

I tried an unlock spell, but the door didn't budge. I tried a stronger one, and the wood creaked, but nothing gave.

"Wiggles, are you up for a little fire magic?" I gestured at the door.

He gave a loud burp, backed up, and opened his mouth. Flames shot against the wooden door, and it was quickly ablaze. The wood splintered and cracked, and after a few seconds, I tried another unlock spell. This time, it worked.

I jumped past what remained of the door and the flames and leaped into Aurora's apartment.

"Oh my..." I blinked several times, unable to believe what I was seeing.

Aurora's gaze met mine, and she bit her bottom lip. She was pinned to the wall by a huge, vibrant green fairy, her wings splayed out in a shimmering wall, preventing Aurora from moving.

Wiggles bounded in and screeched to a halt. "Whoa! Who are you?"

"Yeah, and exactly what are you doing with my sister?" I sparked magic on my fingers, my shock receding as the anger took hold. "You'd better let her go if you don't want to see those pretty wings obliterated."

The fairy bared her sharp teeth and gave a low, guttural laugh. "Hey, losers. Don't you recognize me without my tail?"

"Your... tail?" My gaze ran over the fairy. "I've never met you before, tail or no tail."

Wiggles bounced on the spot. "No way! I know who you are, but it can't be."

"You've met this creature before?" I didn't take my gaze off the fairy.

"I mean, I think so. We both have." Wiggles tilted his head. "That's Bandit."

Chapter 15

I took a step closer, shock still rumbling through me. "Just to be clear, you used to be an annoying ginger cat that demanded to be carried everywhere in Aurora's purse?"

The fairy chortled. "That I was. All that fur! Gah! Don't miss that."

"Aurora, are you okay?" I took another step, inching closer, prepared to take on this fairy if she made one wrong move toward my sister.

She managed a small nod. "Bandit's possessive of me. We developed a strong bond while she was in the form of my cat familiar. I didn't realize how connected we'd become."

My gaze didn't leave the fairy. *This* was what Bandit really looked like? "I'm no threat to Aurora. You should know that. You've been around Wiggles and me plenty of times."

Bandit lowered her wings a few inches. "When I heard the noise downstairs and the door was set on fire, I thought the worst. This village is awash with unstable magic. I need to protect Aurora."

Aurora patted Bandit on one of her large shimmering shoulders. "You can trust Tempest.

Why don't you let me go and we can talk this through?"

"And I've brought brownies," I said.

Bandit launched in the air, swept passed me in a blur of green shimmer and stinging sparkles, and took the bag of brownies with her. She clung to the ceiling as she devoured them.

Aurora raced to my side and grabbed my arm.

"She didn't hurt you, did she?" I whispered.

Aurora shook her head. "Just startled me more than anything. I still don't know how this happened. What happened to my sweet Bandit?"

"It's still me," Bandit said through a mouthful of brownie. "I'm just the new and improved version. Or rather, the old version. The version I've been for over three hundred years. It's nice to be out of that furry body. I can finally fly. My magic is back." To demonstrate, she flared a dazzle of sparks around the apartment.

"We should leave while she's distracted by the food," I said to Aurora.

Bandit moved in a blur of shimmer and crackling sparkles. She stood in front of the fire damaged door, shaking her head as she stuffed another brownie into her mouth. "No one's going anywhere. I'm here to protect Aurora."

"I tried to leave the apartment several times to open the store," Aurora said. "Bandit said it's not safe. Until the stone circle stops malfunctioning, she doesn't want me to move."

I fought my protective urge so as not to charge at this fairy and blast her with magic for keeping Aurora a prisoner. She was still Bandit, and I didn't want anyone to get hurt. Aurora might protect Bandit if I went after her.

"Let's all sit down." Aurora mustered a smile. "I can make us tea."

Bandit shrugged. "Whatever keeps you here is fine by me." Her gaze cut to me. "You're not going to cause me trouble, are you, Tempest? I don't mind you being around, but I won't hesitate in slicing your head off if you cause Aurora problems."

"Slice my..." I glanced at Aurora, who swiftly shook her head. "I'm not going to cause trouble. But Aurora can't stay in here forever."

"Hopefully, we won't need to stay for much longer," Bandit said. "And I can always get provisions." She strode over and shoved me back toward the couch.

"She's very pushy now she's a fairy," Wiggles muttered.

"Be careful, puppy. You look like a ripe juicy plum to me." Bandit scooped Wiggles up and dangled him in front of her mouth. "Maybe I should take a bite."

Wiggles kicked and squirmed, and a blast of flame shot out of his mouth right into Bandit's face.

She extinguished it with a waft of her hand. "Not so clever now, are you, hellhound? I haven't forgotten a single one of your insults. We'll be having words later."

"Bandit! Put Wiggles down," Aurora said, her hands jammed on her hips. "I love him almost as much as I love you."

"I thought I was your favorite?" Wiggles said.

"Let's not discuss that now." Aurora tutted.

After Bandit had glared at Wiggles for a few seconds, she dropped him to the floor.

"I always knew you weren't to be trusted." Wiggles hurried over to me and jumped on the couch.

Aurora rushed over with mugs of tea for everyone and perched next to me, her hands clasped in front of her.

Bandit stood in front of us, her wings extended and a grin on her face. "It's so good to be back."

"When did this change happen?" I asked.

"First thing this morning," Aurora said. "I'd fallen asleep for a few hours after spending a restless night with Bandit. I jumped in the shower quickly while she seemed to be sleeping. When I got out, I heard a rustling in the bedroom."

"My wings." Bandit flicked them. "I forgot how much I loved my wings."

"So, you just... transformed back into a fairy?" My gaze ran over Bandit. "Why?"

"It must be linked to her illness," Aurora said. "The magic was fading and making her feel bad."

"Or it's linked to the stone circle," I said.

A wing flipped through the air, scattering sparkles. "I've not communed with the stones, but I imagine a violent murder would have left them shaken. It could have disturbed the magical vibes of the area, including my own magical balance."

Aurora's bottom lip jutted out. "Does that mean you will remain in your fairy form for good? My cute furry sweetie has gone?"

"Who knows what the stone circle has planned for us? We could all suddenly shift form if that's what the magic decides," I said.

"Please don't turn me into a cat," Wiggles whispered. "I'll be a sloth, a snake, even a snail, just not a cat."

"Hey! Cats are awesome. Although I don't miss the hairballs," Bandit said.

"Maybe now that Bathsheba's killer has been caught, the stone circle will settle and Bandit will change back into a cat," I said.

"The stone circle is still not settled," Aurora said. "I saw bolts of purple light shoot out of the top of it from my window less than an hour ago. And have you seen the color of the sky? Something big is building."

"The problem's solved, though," I said. "Fanny is under arrest. The angels just need to get a confession and charge her."

"I disagree. And your pink sparkly hair and Wiggles' new overripe plum color show that the stone circle hasn't finished with us," Bandit said.

"Hey! I don't look like a plum. And I happen to think puce suits me fine," Wiggles said.

"You don't think... what if the angels have the wrong person for Bathsheba's murder?" Aurora turned to me. "That could be the reason the stone circle is still grouchy."

I shook my head. "It has to be Fanny. She had the motive, opportunity, and the power to kill Bathsheba."

"I should thank her for what she did. My transformation from ginger fur ball to glorious fairy is complete." Bandit fluttered her wings. "Freedom, baby! I love it."

"It could be a delayed reaction," I said. "The stone circle just needs to work through its anger issues."

"Hold that thought." Aurora jumped up and made a move toward her bedroom.

Bandit blocked her path. "Where do you think you're going?"

"Don't worry. I'm not about to leap out the window. I want to see if that weird light is still being shot from the stone circle."

"I'll come with you." Bandit curled her wings around Aurora, and they shuffled into the bedroom.

"That fairy is freaking me out," Wiggles whispered.

"You're not the only one. I can't believe that's the real Bandit."

"I don't like the way she keeps looking at me. I feel like a piece of meat she wants to sauté and take a bite out of."

"I'll bite her if she tries anything funny."

Aurora returned, still partially encased in Bandit's wings. She nudged a wing down. "The stone circle is still angry. There's a constant stream of gray smoke drifting out the top."

I sighed and rubbed the back of my neck. "Setting aside the stone circle for a minute, Bandit, why did you come to Willow Tree Falls in the first place? Are you involved with the Magic Council? You showed up at the same time John Smith's body was found in Abigail's store. Did you follow him here?"

"I don't work for the Magic Council." Bandit's top lip curled as she eased Aurora back into a seat. "They are nothing to me. Fairies have no interest in bureaucracy."

"Then why did you come here? You mentioned our dad." I leaned forward in my seat. "What do you know about him?"

Bandit nodded. "I was sent here on a mission to see both of you. I had the misfortune of being transformed by that uptight Magic Council jerk before I could find you. Our paths crossed, and we clashed. His magic took me by surprise. I've never felt so humiliated when he turned me into a cat."

"I sympathize," Wiggles said. "That is my greatest fear, being feline."

"Your mission was to see us?" Aurora reached over and grabbed my hand. "Why?"

"Did our dad send you here?" My heart thudded like a jackhammer as I waited for the reply.

Bandit nodded. Her features froze, and her hand went to her chest. She coughed. "Gah! It feels like I've got something blocking my airway."

"Tell us about our dad," I said. "Where is he? Is he okay? Does he want to come home? Has his disappearance got something to do with my demon?"

Bandit coughed several times and thumped on her chest. "Give me a minute."

I bit back my frustration. We were so close to finding out the truth.

"We shouldn't push her," Aurora said. "She's been really sick."

"She knows something important." I gestured to Bandit.

"I do. You've got this all wrong." Bandit coughed again.

"Set us straight." I half-stood from my seat.

Bandit's form shimmered. There was a flash of light, and she transformed back into a cat.

Aurora rushed over as Bandit fell to the floor. "Oh! You poor baby. This must be so stressful for you."

"But... but what about our dad?" I hurried over and knelt next to Bandit. "Tell us about him."

Bandit's gaze met mine before she coughed up a hairball and collapsed.

Aurora's hand flew to her mouth. "She's a cat again."

"I thought that's what you wanted."

"Of course, but I don't want her sick again. I'd rather have Bandit as a healthy fairy than a..." a sob shot out, "a dying animal."

I wrinkled my nose as a pungent, decaying smell drifted from Bandit. I lifted one of her paws. She didn't respond. This illness was looking terminal.

"We almost had the information," I said. "Bandit knows something important about Dad."

Aurora sniffed, her full attention on Bandit. "I don't care what it is, so long as she gets better."

"You don't care about Dad?"

Her head shot up. "I do! I mean... oh, this is all such a mess. I want Bandit well, Dad home, and for the stone circle to leave us alone."

"None of those are easy tasks." I blew out a breath.

"Do you really think the stone circle did this to Bandit?" Aurora asked.

"It has to be connected. Bathsheba is killed, the stone circle goes crazy, Bandit gets sick, and then her form shifts. Nothing we've tried has been able to transform her."

"Then you need to solve this murder and fast, or my Bandit may never return to me, and we'll never find out what her message about Dad is."

I sat back on my heels, my mind whirling with the possibilities.

"Tempest, what are you going to do?" Aurora tugged on my sleeve. "Bandit needs to get better. It makes my heart hurt seeing her so weak."

"You still want Bandit around, knowing what she's really like?" I asked.

Aurora's forehead wrinkled. "Of course. I mean, she's a little over possessive and scary to look at until you get used to her, but she's still my sweet little Bandit under all the shimmering wings."

"Not to mention the razor-sharp teeth and her desire to eat me," Wiggles muttered.

"She'll be fine when she gets used to you," Aurora said.

"You can't keep an enormous, powerful, possessive fairy around," I said. "It's not safe for you, and it's not safe for anyone here."

"Now's not the time to discuss that," Aurora said. "If the stone circle is still misbehaving because Bathsheba's killer is still out there, how are you going to find out who really killed her?"

I rapped my knuckles together. "I was so sure it was Fanny."

Lightning dazzled me. It was followed by a loud clap of thunder right overhead.

"Can we assume that was the stone circle giving you a message?" Aurora asked.

I tipped my head back. "Give me one flash of lightning to tell me Fanny is innocent. Two flashes to say she's guilty."

A single, clear line of lightning blazed across the sky.

"Wow! The stone circle is talking to you," Aurora said.

"And it's telling me I'm wrong about Fanny." I ran a hand down my face. "We have to go back to basics and return to the scene of the crime. Something was missed. If Fanny didn't sneak into that tent and kill Bathsheba, and it wasn't the two guys who robbed her, it must have been someone already inside the tent."

"A member of her family killed her?"

There was a huge, earth trembling boom of thunder.

I nodded. "We just have to figure out if it was Liam, Charlotte, or Picasso."

Chapter 16

"Are you sure you should stay here?" I pulled Aurora closer, just in case Bandit woke and overheard us. "We can sneak you out right now."

"I can't leave Bandit in this condition," Aurora said.

"What if she wakes and turns into a murderous-minded fairy again? This could be your only chance to get away."

"She was only acting like that after you arrived. She heard the break-in in the store and thought the worst. Before that, she was being sweet, in a sort of overly possessive and mildly terrifying way. You know what fairies are like."

"Dangerous, not to be trusted, and likely to blind you with their glitter?"

Aurora tutted. "They aren't all so bad."

"I don't want you to be on your own with her," I said.

"And I'm not leaving her," Aurora said. "Bandit may have issues, but she's still my familiar. I can't abandon her because things have gotten difficult. That's like you abandoning Wiggles because he ate too many cupcakes."

"That's a totally different thing. Would you consider abandoning her if she tried to kill you?"

"It won't come to that." Aurora led Wiggles and me down the stairs and opened the store door. "Now get out of here and deal with this murder. The sooner you solve it and the right person is arrested, the happier the stone circle will be, and the village can get back to normal. Maybe Bandit will remain in her cat form when the stones are quiet."

After shooting one more look around Aurora's store, I headed out with Wiggles. I wasn't happy to leave her, but Aurora had her own powers. I couldn't always hover around her. That made me as bad as Bandit.

Jeez, Bandit was now a terrifying, powerful fairy! I wasn't sure I could get used to that.

"This theory had better be right," I said to Wiggles. "What if the stone circle isn't playing up because of the murder?"

"You think the stones are broken for good?"

"It could be something more serious affecting the stability of the village." I shook my head. One thing at a time. Solve the murder first and then see what happens. If this didn't work, it might be time to take a long vacation.

A chaotic mess greeted Wiggles and me as we walked through the front door of Angel Force.

The waiting room chairs were full, with villagers looking shocked, angry, or injured.

There was an argument going on at the front desk, and someone was being restrained and shoved into the back room toward the cells.

I dodged past the arguing group and into the main office.

Angels whizzed backward and forward, looking as out of control as the rest of the village.

It took me a moment, but I spotted Dazielle at the back of the office, her lips pressed together and her wings outstretched.

I hurried over and nudged my way past several angels waiting to get her attention.

Her gaze flicked to me. "Not now, Tempest. As you can see, we've got a situation here."

"And you'll have more situations if you don't arrest the right person for Bathsheba's murder."

She turned to me. "What are you talking about? We have the right person. Everyone agrees that Fanny killed Bathsheba."

"I don't, not anymore."

Dazielle closed her eyes and squeezed the bridge of her nose. "You had everyone convinced it was her. I agreed with you. Everything points to Fanny."

"Even I was convinced it was her," I said. "But the stone circle is still malfunctioning. And Bandit said—"

"Aurora's familiar? You're taking advice from a ginger ball of fur with an attitude almost as bad as Wiggles?"

"I'm nothing like that cat," Wiggles said, turning his attention from an abandoned plate of cookies.

"Yeah, Bandit's a bit more than your average cat, but that's a story for another time," I said. "I've got an idea about how we can figure out who killed Bathsheba."

"Tempest, you're out of your depth on this case. If you keep going like this, you'll have accused every person in the village of killing Bathsheba." Dazielle turned to walk away, but I hurried in front of her and blocked her path.

"Give me thirty minutes. It's got to be one of three people. Someone inside the tent is the murderer. That means it was either Bathsheba's husband, Liam, or one of her children."

"Why do you think it was one of them? Why not Fanny?"

"Because the chaos in the village is getting worse," I said. "I think the stone circle wants this murder solved even more than you do. The stones aren't happy. If they could talk, they'd tell us we had the wrong person in custody. Instead, they're showing us by disrupting the magic."

Her gaze drifted over my pink hair. "You only think, or you know for certain that's the case?"

I lifted a shoulder. "I'm eighty percent sure."

"That's not good enough." Dazielle gestured around the room. "I have dozens of open cases to deal with. I can't work based on your hunches."

"Solve this murder and you'll get all the cases closed," I said. "This chaos will disappear once the stones are happy." I matched her step as she tried to dodge around me. "Bathsheba's murder was the triggering incident that destabilized the stones. Let's fix that problem and see if it helps."

"And if it doesn't? Would you be willing to go up against the stone circle?"

"Go up against... the stones? No one would survive that. I'm not going on a suicide mission to prove a point."

"That's what I figured." Dazielle snorted and shoved me to one side. "I don't have time for your wild theories."

"This isn't a wild theory." I grabbed hold of her wing and yanked on it to get her attention. "We need to recreate the crime scene."

Dazielle grabbed my hand and twisted hard until I let go of her feathers. "Why would we do that?"

"It'll show us where everybody was at the time of the murder. The tent's still up. All we need are the suspects. We position them in the locations they were in when the killing took place. That'll show us who was in the best position to fire the magic at Bathsheba."

"No! Fanny's in custody. She's my prime suspect. She's not hiding her hatred for Bathsheba. She's practically confessed to the killing."

My eyebrows shot up. "She has?"

Dominic stood behind Dazielle, his wings ruffling around him as he scratched his chin. "Um, sorry to disagree with you, boss. Fanny said she'd have loved to have killed Bathsheba, but not that she'd actually done it."

Irritation traced across Dazielle's face. "Which is almost a confession."

"That's not true. I get that Fanny hated Bathsheba, but why be so open about it if she'd actually killed her? Surely, she'd do the opposite to make sure no one suspected her. It's not Fanny," I said. "Everyone we need to recreate the crime scene is still in the village, but they won't be here much longer. Charlotte and Picasso are leaving today. If we don't grab them now, it'll be too late. We may never solve this murder. If we don't, the stone circle will continue to act up."

Dazielle advanced toward me, her wings outstretched. "You need to leave. You're causing another problem for me, and I have enough of those."

"Half an hour, that's all I need. We grab the suspects, set up the crime scene, and re-enact it."

"You've been wrong before when it comes to this case. Why will this time be any different?"

I lifted a hand. "I'll admit I jumped on the likelihood that it was Mack and Coleman who'd killed Bathsheba."

"And then Fanny."

"Sure. Then Fanny. She looked good for it. But now—"

"You're wildly jabbing a finger at somebody else," Dazielle said. "You don't know what you're talking about. Get out of my station."

The floor underneath our feet rumbled, and the overhead lights flickered.

"You see! That's the stone circle telling you I'm right," I said.

"You think the stones are on your side?" Dazielle shook her head. "The stone circle is looking out for itself. Once we get the confession out of Fanny, they'll stop overreacting."

The lights blinked out, the station walls vibrated, and a bolt of lightning slammed through the ceiling, narrowly missing Dazielle.

I leaped back, Wiggles jumping into my arms as I did so. The air crackled around us, and my hair flew about with all the static. "If that's not a sign, I don't know what else to say. Dazielle, give this a try. We just need a bit of time and the suspects."

She picked herself up off the floor, shooing away the outstretched hands of her angels. Her feathers trembled as she smoothed down her hair. "Maybe we should try it your way."

I worked really hard not to smirk as I set Wiggles back on the floor. "Good idea."

"It'll take time to assemble the suspects," Dazielle said. "And going so close to the stone circle in its unstable state is a risk. We'll need additional angels to stand guard."

"I'm prepared to take that risk if it solves this problem," I said.

Dazielle sighed. "This will take valuable resources from the other problems in the village. If you're wrong about this—"

"I'm not. And bill me for the angels' overtime if you like," I said. "Although if I solve this, I'll consider the debt paid."

She nodded curtly. "Very well. While the angels gather the suspects, and I pull my resources back to the station, how about you do something useful?"

"What do you need me to do?"

"Apologize to Oriel. You haven't been to see her according to the hospital records."

"Oh, I've been meaning to. I've been... busy." A trickle of guilt ran through me. I hadn't forgotten about the injured angel, but with everything going on in the village and the issues with Bandit, it had slipped my mind.

"Go see her and apologize for what you did," Dazielle said. "It might help her recovery."

"Now? We're dealing with a crisis situation and you want me to sit by a sick angel's bedside."

"You're no use to me here. You and that thieving hellhound will get in my way while I'm trying to work." She grabbed Wiggles and extracted a cherry bun from his mouth.

"Hey! I was enjoying that." Wiggles stomped away, glaring at Dazielle as she tossed the bun in the trash.

"Cut him some slack. He stress eats," I said.

"You owe Oriel, Tempest. You owe me. And if you stay here, that will keep happening." She jabbed a finger over my shoulder. "I don't need my angels anymore stressed than they already are."

I turned. Wiggles was already hunkered under a desk, his gaze on an angel who was eating a cookie. "Fine, we'll leave. Just keep an open mind about doing this. You might be in for a pleasant surprise."

"Nothing is pleasant when it comes to you. Now get out of here before I change my mind." Dazielle arched an eyebrow. "And in case you'd forgotten, the hospital is half a mile due east."

"Of course, I hadn't forgotten." I grumbled as I hurried out of the station with Wiggles.

"We should get cake," he said.

"I think Oriel is still unconscious," I said. "She won't appreciate it."

"I meant for us," he said. "Being inside that station has rocketed my stress levels. I can't believe Dazielle stopped me from enjoying that cherry bun.

She threw it in the trash! Those angels need to take a chill pill."

"They're not used to hard work." I glanced over my shoulder, doubt stirring inside me. "This crime scene re-enactment had better work. If it doesn't, I'm all out of ideas."

"It will," Wiggles said. "Once we get cake, everything will seem so much brighter."

Our swift hunt for cake wasn't a success. Sprinkles was closed, Unicorn's Trough looked like no one had been in there for days, and even Tilly's restaurant was shut. It appeared everyone was hunkering down and hoping the stone circle would sort itself out.

I dashed back to Cloven Hoof, hunted through the kitchen cupboards, and discovered a tub of peanut butter and raisin cookies. With tub in hand, we raced over to the hospital.

More disorder greeted us as we got inside. The waiting room was full, heaving with bleary-eyed and shocked patients waiting to be seen.

Magic was excellent at healing minor injuries, but anything more serious needed a specialist. We only had one doctor in the village and three part-time nurses. It looked like they were stretched to the breaking point.

I stopped at the hospital reception desk. Virginia Mackenzie was on duty, trying to placate a wide-eyed individual with a large bandage wrapped around his head who was demanding to see the doctor.

She turned her round face to me and pushed her dark curls out of the way. "Get that dog out of here."

Virginia pointed at Wiggles. "This is a hospital, not a stray pound. It's not hygienic to have animals here."

"Of course." I winked at Wiggles. "Go wait outside."

The second Virginia's back was turned, Wiggles doubled back and crab-walked on his belly past the reception desk, where he hid beside a vending machine out of her line of sight.

"Are you injured too?" Virginia turned back to me.

"Nope, I'm in perfect health."

"Then what are you doing here?"

"I'm here to see Oriel," I said. "Which room is she in?"

"End of the corridor, room number twelve. I didn't know you were friendly with her."

"It's more of a courtesy call," I said.

"Don't get in the way of our work while you're here," Virginia said.

I lifted a hand as I backed away from the reception. "You won't even know I've been here."

I sidestepped several injured people as I headed along the corridor and collected Wiggles. It looked like people were arriving from a war zone, with bloody bandages on injured limbs and trolleys loaded with unconscious people being shoved into treatment rooms. The stone circle was getting out of hand.

I pushed through a closed door and found Oriel's room. I was met by a peaceful calm as the door slid shut behind me, the chaos contained out in the corridor.

I peered at the gray-skinned angel. I'd never seen an angel who wasn't drop dead gorgeous. This one looked more like a corpse than a light-filled being intent on administering righteous justice.

"Hi there. I'm Tempest Crypt. You must be Oriel." I set the tub of cookies on the side table by the bed.

"I've never seen her before." Wiggles placed his paws on the bed and studied the angel.

"I'm guessing not many people have," I said. "If she spent the last two decades hidden inside Angel Force, then no one will know her."

"That's just weird," Wiggles said. "What's so important about the evidence room?"

"All the evidence to put the criminals away," I said.

"But how boring. This angel never went to an after-work party or took a lunchtime stroll in the sun and grabbed a triple chocolate muffin and a hot chocolate. That's not much of a life. I feel sorry for her."

I scrutinized the angel. She was smaller than the others, although that could simply be because her wings were tucked out of sight. Most angels stood well over six feet tall, were broad-shouldered with manes of luxurious blonde hair. This one was small, squat, and her blonde hair was more strawberry-colored. Maybe she was what the angels considered the runt of the litter, so she didn't like to go out in public for fear of humiliation.

Still, for a runt, she was impressive looking. I was certain that, once the death pallor was gone, she'd be super cute.

I walked around the room. There was nothing to look at. The walls were painted white, and other than two chairs in one corner, the bed the angel lay on, and the side table, there was nothing else in the room.

I pulled up a chair. "So, why aren't you waking up? Dazielle's trying to blame me for this. Well, I guess it was sort of my fault, but I didn't know you'd be in the evidence room. No one was supposed to get hurt."

"Do you think she can hear you?" Wiggles asked.

"Maybe. I don't know," I said. "Better to talk to myself than sit in silence."

"Try a cookie," Wiggles said. "Hold it under her nose. When you do that to me, it always wakes me up, no matter how deeply asleep I am."

"That's true. But you can smell a cookie at a thousand paces," I said.

"Try it. And while you're at it, you can throw me one," he said.

I took a cookie from out of the tub and wafted it under Oriel's nose. There was no reaction.

I bit off a piece of the cookie before tossing the rest to Wiggles. "I'm sorry for what happened to you. I was promised it would be a quick in and out job. No one would be injured. If I knew that you lived in the evidence room, I'd have never told Isaac how to get in. I messed up. I hope you can forgive me."

Oriel didn't move. Other than her chest rising and falling slowly, there was no response.

I sat back in my seat. "I wonder what hobbies she has."

"I'm guessing she likes cataloging evidence and sitting in gloomy rooms on her own," Wiggles said.

"There's more to life than that," I said. "Do you think she's dating anyone?"

"I doubt there are many guys interested in angels who never leave their home."

"She could have someone waiting for her," I said. Although the lack of get well soon cards or gifts suggested she didn't have a big friendship group.

"We should sing to her," Wiggles said. "Isn't music good for coma patients?"

"Not the way we sing." I shook my head. "I'm going to have words with Isaac. This wasn't the deal we made."

"I blame Dazielle," Wiggles said. "She shouldn't be hiding an angel in the evidence room in the first place."

I took another cookie and wafted it under Oriel's nose again. Still no response. Wiggles got that one as well.

"What else can I do to get her to wake up?" I looked at Wiggles. "I said I'm sorry."

"Did you really mean it?" Wiggles said.

"Of course! Come on. Let's get out of here. We've got a crime scene to re-enact. The angels have had enough time to pull the suspects together." I stood and placed the chair back in its original position.

I returned to the bed and stared down at Oriel. "I hope you get better soon. If there's anything I can do, you know, to make up for how things played out, let me know. Of course, to do that, you need to open your eyes, so that's going to be tricky." I gave the back of her hand a quick pat.

A blast of brilliant white light shot out of Oriel's mouth and arced over the bed before hitting the floor.

I staggered away, my back hitting the wall.

"What's she doing?" Wiggles stared at Oriel, his hackles raised and his eyes glowing.

"I have no idea." I stared at the beam of light. It flickered for a few seconds before stabilizing.

"Congratulations! I didn't know if you'd figure this one out, Tempest."

"Whoa! Hold up now! That's Isaac's voice," I said.

"You came through for me with the evidence room. Shame about this angel being there when we arrived. You forgot to mention that little speed bump," he said through the beam of light.

I pursed my lips. "I bet you're weeping about it into your whiskey every night."

There was a pause. "I've got an update for you. I figured I'd use the assets I had at my disposal to pass it on."

I stepped closer to the bed. This was all Isaac's doing? He put Oriel into a deep sleep to give me a message? He was one twisted son of a gun.

"Your dad was seen recently in Puzzlewood. Just to warn you, he wasn't in the best of shape. You might find him there if you don't wait around for too long. Better to go there than the Dark Realm. Oh, and Tempest, you owe me one for this. I don't forget."

The light shooting out of Oriel's mouth faded.

My hand went to my stomach. My head felt woozy as I processed this information. Dad was in

Puzzlewood? It would be easy to find him there and bring him home.

Oriel groaned. Her eyes flickered open. "Where... what... what's going on?"

I sucked in a breath. "I need to go."

"Wait!" Oriel looked at me with wide eyes. "Who are you? Where am I?"

"Everything's great. You're in the hospital. You were involved in a... accident. I'm really sorry about that, by the way. I'll get a doctor to come see you, but I've got to leave." I jerked my head at Wiggles, and we raced out the door. Excitement and nerves bubbled through me. I'd just found out where my dad was.

Now all I had to do was get him back.

Chapter 17

I stopped the doctor on my way out and quickly told him the patient in room twelve was awake before racing out of the hospital.

I had to tell someone what had just happened. This was amazing news. Puzzlewood was safe and accessible. Magic users went there on their holidays. It was great fun for children. If Dad was there, it meant things couldn't be so bad for him.

It would be no problem to get there, find Dad, and bring him home. We might even be able to get him back by the end of the day.

I resisted the urge to skip, opting instead for a jog as we headed to Aurora's store to tell her this amazing news.

"Do you believe that message?" Wiggles asked as he trotted along beside me.

"Of course. Why lie to me about this?" I asked.

"Because it's Isaac Dubrov," Wiggles said. "He's not known to be a straight up and down kind of guy."

"There was no point in him leaving me that message," I said.

"There was if he calls in that favor. He doesn't give something for nothing."

I was too excited to worry about that. "Things are going in the right direction. Oriel's awake, which will make Dazielle happy, we have a new lead on Dad, and once we solve this murder—"

Wiggles dodged in front of me and blocked my path. "I know this is great news, but think about what just happened for a second."

I dodged past him, but he jumped in my way again.

"What's your problem? I've got news about Dad. Why aren't you happy about it?"

"I am. But you haven't seen him for years." Wiggles planted a paw on my leg. "What will he be like after all this time?"

"The... well, he'll be the same," I said. "Older, of course. Just because he's been away from us for a while doesn't change anything. He's still my dad. He'll still love Aurora and me."

"Sure, he will," Wiggles said. "After all, you're both adorable. But how will everyone else feel? What about your mom?"

I bit my bottom lip as a jolt of unease hit. I'd been so involved in thinking about how amazing it would be to get my dad back that I hadn't stopped to think about everyone else's feelings. "It might take a bit of getting used to. We need to know why Dad left in the first place. I need to know most of all. If he left because of Frank, that's something we'll have to deal with. And I will. I'll fix all of this. Make things right for everyone."

"Maybe your mom wants the past left where it is," Wiggles said.

"Why? She still loves him. She's not even dated since Dad left."

"That doesn't mean she'll be happy to see him back. Maybe he left because there was a problem between them."

I jammed my hands on my hips. "I... I don't know the answer to that. Mom doesn't talk about him anymore. That doesn't mean she won't be happy to have news about him."

"No doubt. It might be worth giving her a heads-up before chasing after this," Wiggles said. "At least she'll be prepared if you bring him home."

"And if I go find him and he's not there, I'll have gotten her hopes up for no reason. I don't want to break her heart all over again. She hides it well, but she was devastated when he disappeared."

"I think it's worth the risk," Wiggles said.

I blew out a breath and tipped my head back. Dark, storm-laden clouds glared back at me. "I just want everything back to normal. I want the village safe again, I want Bandit to not transform into some scary-eyed fairy who wants to eat you, and I want my dad back home where he belongs." Everything felt so close but still frustratingly out of reach.

"Far be it for me to act like the sensible one in this relationship," Wiggles said, "but you need to share this. What if your mom knows something about why your dad vanished? Maybe why you shouldn't be so quick to get him back home."

"Mom wouldn't have kept that from me," I said. "She knew how hard Aurora and I took it when he left."

"She may have done it for your own good," he said. "If he had anything to do with Frank coming into your life and he needed to keep everyone safe, she'd guard that secret with her life."

I tapped a finger against my forehead. "Let's head to the house and see who's around. But Mom's not talking me out of this. I am going to Puzzlewood and getting Dad back. And since we're running out of time, let's do this the quick way." I scooped Wiggles into my arms and performed a translocation spell, dropping us outside the front door of the family home.

I set Wiggles down and pushed open the front door. "Mom! Are you home?" I headed straight into the kitchen where she could usually be found, but there was no one there. Granny Dottie's black familiar opened one eye and peered at me before shutting it again.

"Where is everyone?" I turned in a circle. It felt like no one had been here for a while. There was no food on the stove, and everything was quiet, the air undisturbed.

I checked the back garden, all the upstairs bedrooms, and every room downstairs. The place was empty.

Disquiet ran through me as I headed to the front door. The demon prison could still be acting up. Maybe everyone was over there. I dashed out the house and raced over to the cemetery with Wiggles hot on my heels.

Unusually, the double gates were wide open. I stepped over the threshold and paused.

Wiggles remained outside the gate and whimpered.

"What's the matter with you?" I asked.

"I don't like the feel of this place," he said. "Something's really off in the prison."

"Just like the rest of the village," I said. "We need to get in and find everybody."

A light fog drifted around the cemetery, and the moisture soaked into my hair and clothes.

I strode around the perimeter of the cemetery, getting a feel for the place and checking for cracks. It was too quiet, like the place was waiting to exhale something foul all over me the second I put a foot wrong.

When I'd seen Granny Dottie at Cloven Hoof, she'd said the demons had been misbehaving, but now it felt as if they weren't even here.

My gut clenched, and I knelt, placing both hands on the ground. The familiar thrum of protective magic pulsed through me. The barriers and binding spells were in place. The demons hadn't gotten out, but where was everybody? And why were the demons being so quiet? Could they be scared of the stone circle? If a hoard of out of control, dark demons were scared of what was going on in the village, I needed to be terrified.

I hurried over to the crypt Granny Dottie used for her serious thinking time. The door was shut. It was usually open whenever anyone patrolled the cemetery. It was a handy place to hide in if the weather turned bad or you wanted a break.

I touched the stone and winced. It felt hot. I grabbed the handle and tugged it, but it wouldn't move.

"What are you doing?"

I jumped as Wiggles appeared beside me. "I thought you were too scared to come into the cemetery?"

"I found an endless depth of courage from somewhere." He shivered. "Where is everyone?"

"Hiding or missing. And someone's done something weird to this crypt. It doesn't want to open."

A crackle of purple magic spat from a headstone and zapped Wiggles on the nose.

He jumped away and rubbed his nose on the damp grass. "Ouch! Not funny."

"None of this is funny." A cold ball of worry lodged inside me. "This is weird. Where's everyone hiding?"

"More importantly, what are they hiding from?" Wiggles glanced over his shoulder. "Nothing scares your family."

The fog around us grew colder and denser as I stared at the sealed crypt. The demon prison was rarely left unattended. Only on special occasions and for short periods of time was it left without anyone keeping an eye on things.

I backed up and fired several unlock and reveal spells at the crypt. It took several rounds of magic before the stone grated open.

Wiggles poked his head in before backpedaling and bumping into my legs. "Eek! You need to see this."

I pulled the door open wider. "What the—" Everyone was inside the crypt. Mom, Auntie Queenie, Granny Dottie, Grandpa Lucius, and

Uncle Kenny. They lay on their backs, their hands resting on their chests.

I raced over to Mom and knelt beside her. She was breathing, but she was ice cold.

"Mom! Wake up." I tapped her cheek.

She didn't respond.

I tried everyone, but got the same response. They were out for the count, cold, gray-skinned, and unresponsive.

Panic gripped me, and my throat tightened. "What's going on here?" I shivered as the icy fog drifted in and wrapped around me.

"Did they do this to themselves?" Wiggles asked. "Are they protecting themselves from something lurking outside?"

"No one's powerful enough to bring down the whole family," I said. "I don't get why they are in here. What spell are they under? And why seal the crypt?"

I coughed as I inhaled a lungful of the icy fog. My head grew woozy, and I staggered to the side, my hand reaching out for the stone wall to stop from falling.

"What's wrong with you?" Wiggles asked.

I took in another deep breath, and the cold tickled the back of my throat along with a bitter tang. The fog swirled into the crypt at an alarming rate.

My eyes widened, and I clamped a hand over my mouth. "We need to get out of here." My voice was muffled as I scooped Wiggles up in my free hand and hurried out of the crypt.

I blasted a spell at the stone door to force it back into place and stop the fog from getting in. Then I turned and raced out of the cemetery, my vision blurry and my head feeling heavy. My lungs burned as they willed me to take a breath, but if I did that, it might be my last.

I crashed out through the gates and landed on my knees.

Wiggles jumped from my arms and turned to stare at me. "That was... interesting."

I pointed back over my shoulder as I sucked in a longed-for breath of air that didn't taste of ice and bitter lemons. "It's the fog. Didn't you feel it?"

His ears pricked. "It felt wet."

"It's got something in it."

"Poisonous fog?"

"Or spell tainted with something nasty." I shuffled onto my knees. "You're lower than me. Maybe you didn't breathe much in, so it didn't affect you." My senses snapped back into clarity as the noxious swirling nastiness left my body.

"Someone sent a toxic fog across the cemetery?" Wiggles peered into the swirling, gloomy fog.

"Or something did. I'm thinking our attacker is probably big, gray, and made of stone. This is the work of the stone circle. When the fog got into the cemetery, everyone must have hunted for cover and sealed themselves in the crypt to stop the fog from getting them."

Wiggles backed away from the gates. "We need to do the same. That fog is coming after us."

I staggered to my feet and turned. Thin fingers of fog swirled out of the gates. I blasted them closed and covered them in a protective magic seal. "That won't hold it for long. The fog will seep out of any cracks it finds."

"It's looking for its next victim," Wiggles said.

"And that won't be us." I raced with Wiggles back to Angel Force.

The same bedlam we'd encountered earlier met us as we pushed through the doors.

Dazielle was surrounded by yelling villagers, demanding answers and wanting an end to the chaos the stone circle was causing.

I shoved past them and grabbed her elbow. "We have another problem."

She glowered down at me. "Add it to the list."

"It needs to go to the top. I've just encountered poisonous fog. This isn't a joke. That fog has my family passed out in the cemetery. There's no one around to keep the demons in check."

She jerked back then cleared her throat. "We can't have the demons loose. If the prison is compromised -"

"The fog is our biggest threat right now. You need to get the villagers out of here. Send them home. Make sure they don't let that fog near them."

Dazielle's gaze skittered around the crowded waiting room. "Are you sure about this?"

"I almost passed out after taking in a single breath of the stuff. Every other Crypt witch is out cold. This fog isn't playing."

She nodded before sucking in a breath and raising her hands. "Everyone listen to me. You must return to your homes and seal yourself in. Block all airways."

The crowd around her was silent for a few seconds, then the yelling and panic began.

Dazielle extended her wings and flitted over the crowd. "Go home now or be arrested. This is a matter of life or death. Leave!"

The crowd scattered, and within a few seconds, the reception area was empty.

I blew out a breath as Dazielle alighted on the floor. "I'm seriously impressed."

She shrugged. "Sometimes you have to be cruel to be kind. Where's this fog?"

"Seeping out of the cemetery. My family is trapped inside a crypt."

"And it's coming this way?"

"It's just getting started. Are you ready to solve this murder? If we get this right, it should make the stone circle happy and stop trying to kill us all."

Her narrowed gaze cut to me before she nodded. "I'm willing to try anything."

"So, let's go re-enact the crime scene. Have you still got Fanny in custody?"

"Yes, and Mack and Coleman are in the cells. My angels have collected Charlotte, Picasso, and Liam, and I have six angels available to stand guard and watch the stone circle."

"Then we have everything we need." I turned to the door, but she stopped me.

"The prison. Are the demons at risk of escape?"

"Not yet. The magic is holding, but I can't guarantee how long that'll last. The sooner we figure out this murder, the better."

"Dominic and Jophiel," Dazielle yelled, "collect the suspects. Bring them to the tent by the stone circle."

The angels flew into action.

"I need to use your snow globe. Aurora wasn't in the crypt. She must still be at her store. I have to warn her not to leave."

"Be quick." Dazielle gestured to the globe on the reception desk.

I activated it with a shake and pressed my finger on it. "Connect me to Aurora Crypt."

It took a few seconds, but her face appeared. "Tempest! Where are you?"

"With the angels. Listen, you must stay inside. There's a toxic fog spreading through the village."

"A what?"

"No time to explain. Stay inside, keep all the windows shut, and block any cracks."

"I... of course. Is everyone else okay?"

I decided to tell a tiny lie. It was for her benefit. "They're great. Safe at the cemetery. How's Bandit?"

"Still the same. She hasn't stirred."

"We need to move," Dazielle said.

I nodded. "Aurora, I'm heading to the stone circle now. This is almost over."

"Stay safe."

"You too." I ended the link and shut my eyes for a second.

"This had better work, Tempest," Dazielle said.

"It will." I hoped I sounded more positive than I felt. If I didn't solve this soon, the chances were, none of us would get out of this village alive.

Chapter 18

"I don't understand why we all have to be here." Liam entered the tent, closely followed by Charlotte and Picasso, who both had scowls on their faces.

I stood in the middle of the main living room of the tent, Dazielle beside me.

Liam frowned when he spotted us. "Why have your angels brought us here? I demand answers."

"We're doing a re-enactment of your wife's murder," I said. "Whoever killed Bathsheba is still free. We need to discover who that is. Otherwise, the stone circle will never settle."

"We don't care about your stone circle," Liam said. "It's not as if we live here."

"You're a magic user. You must want to ensure our magic isn't revealed to the rest of the world. If a hole gets blasted through the magical barrier, people will start asking questions. That's when trouble will start for all of us. You don't want that, do you?"

The ground beneath our feet rumbled as if the stone circle prompted Liam to an answer.

He glanced over his shoulder. "Of course not. But... I mean, this has nothing to do with us."

The ground quivered again.

"If the stone circle isn't happy with you, you might not get a chance to leave the village at all," I said.

"That's nonsense. I can leave whenever I like." Liam turned to the exit but was blocked by two angels.

"Settle down everyone," Dazielle said. "This won't take long." She glanced at me and nodded.

It was time to get this re-enactment going. "Everyone either sit or stand in the places you were the night Bathsheba was killed," I said.

"Why is that important?" Charlotte asked.

"So we can figure out exactly what happened in here."

"We already know what happened," Liam said. "You have Fanny in custody. She killed Bathsheba."

"They're not holding me anymore." Fanny walked through the opening of the tent, two angels on either side of her.

Liam's eyes widened. "They're letting you go? You didn't kill Bathsheba?"

"Fanny's still in our custody for now," Dazielle said.

"Even though I'm innocent," she said quietly. "Do you really believe the angels, Liam? Do you think I'm a killer?"

He stuttered out a few words before raking a hand through his hair. "Well, I mean, you didn't like her."

"Name me one person who did like her," she said. Her gaze went around the room. "None of you thought much of the late great Bathsheba Delaware. You tolerated her because of her money and influence, but that was about it."

"That's not true," Picasso said. "She was our mom."

Fanny shook her head. "All I know is that I'm innocent. I didn't kill Bathsheba. I certainly thought about it plenty of times, but I didn't do it. However, I would like to find the person responsible, so I can congratulate them."

"That's enough," Dazielle said. "Murder is never something to admire."

Fanny sniffed and looked away.

"Let's get everyone into place." I gestured to the seats.

Charlotte and Picasso exchanged a glance before they settled in the chairs by the door.

"Where were you, Liam?" I turned to him.

"Standing by Bathsheba's left shoulder," he said. "She was sitting in the gold chair. That was her favorite seat."

"Go stand over there," I said.

"Who's going to be Bathsheba?" Liam asked.

I glanced at Dazielle. "Would you do the honors?"

"Is that really necessary?"

"It'll make it more authentic if someone is in the murder seat. You're a bit taller than Bathsheba, but it should work."

Her lips pursed, but she nodded, headed over to the seat, and settled in it.

Mack and Coleman appeared in the tent doorway.

"What's going on here?" Mack asked. "You can't still think we're involved."

"Only when it comes to the robbery," I said.

"Unless you have something else you'd like to confess to." Dazielle leaned forward in the seat, her fierce gaze pinned to the men.

Mack shook his head. "We're cooperating. The angels said you'd be lenient on us if we did this."

"We'll be something like that," I said. "You came in the back of the tent when you robbed Bathsheba, is that right?"

Coleman nodded. "We did. There's a back way in, which we snuck through. It was open, so it was simple to get in."

"And whoever told you about the jewels Bathsheba was carrying also informed you where you'd find them?"

"That's right," Coleman said. "There are sleeping quarters at the back of the tent and a case where most of the jewels were kept."

"Yeah, but we were told the most expensive jewels would be worn by Bathsheba, which is why we came through," Mack said.

"Greedy underhanded sneaks," Liam muttered.

"Hey, buddy, less of the self-righteous comments. We didn't marry someone old enough to be our mother to get our hands on some cash," Coleman said.

Liam jerked his head back. "Bathsheba wasn't old enough to be my mother."

"Yeah, not by much," Mack said. "I know what I'd prefer to do."

Muffled cries came from outside the tent. Dazielle stood and strode to the door. She poked her head out before turning and looking at me. "Carry on. I'll be back in a moment." She disappeared through the tent flap.

"Mack and Coleman, position yourselves at the back of the tent," I said. "Stand where you were when you first came in and demanded the jewels Bathsheba wore."

They muttered between themselves for a few seconds before walking over, accompanied by angels.

I looked around the group and gave a nod. Someone in here murdered Bathsheba. I glanced at Fanny.

She raised her eyebrows. "Don't look at me for this murder. I wasn't here. I was probably halfway back to the hotel when it happened."

"Stay by the main entrance for now. Don't move unless I tell you to," I said.

She shrugged. "I'm more than happy not to be involved in this."

Dazielle strode back through the tent entrance. She caught hold of my arm and dragged me outside. "You need to see something."

I pulled my arm out of her painful grip. "What's going on?"

"That's going on." She pointed to the circle of angels surrounding the tent. Several were sagging forward, their hands braced against their knees and their wings drooping. Two of them were on their knees as the fog drifted around them, looking for a way through and into the tent.

"I thought your angels were made of strong stuff."

Dazielle clicked her tongue against the roof of her mouth. "Whatever's in that fog, it's dangerous. My angels can only hold it off for a few more minutes. Once it gets to us, that's it."

I licked my lips as the thick bank of angry swirling fog inched closer. This really was make or break time. "Then we'd better get back inside and re-enact this murder." I turned and ran back in the tent with Dazielle.

Everyone stared at us with wide eyes as we entered.

"What's going on out there?" Coleman asked. "What's with the weird fog we saw when we were dragged here?"

"Don't mind that," I said. "Dazielle, get back in the chair and play Bathsheba."

She settled in the seat. "Now what?"

"Mack and Coleman, show us what you did when you came in the tent. You grabbed the jewelry from the box in the sleeping quarters, and then you came through here. Then what?" I asked.

Mack shrugged. "I demanded Bathsheba hand over her jewelry."

"And what did she say?" I asked.

"Everyone seemed shocked. Then she got angry and told us to go away or she'd have us arrested."

"She was right snooty about it too. Called us dirty old beggars," Coleman said.

"We weren't going until we got what we wanted," Mack said. "That jewelry was worth a small fortune. We could have taken a year off and had a holiday somewhere sunny."

"So, Bathsheba handed over her jewelry—"

"After complaining about it," Coleman said.

"That's hardly a surprise," Liam said. "You robbed her. She had a right to be angry."

"Go on," I said to Mack. "Then what?"

"We were about to leave," Mack said, "when there was this clicking sound. That's when everything went dark."

I nodded. "Someone used a spell to remove all sources of light in the tent."

"That's when the blast of white light hit Bathsheba," Coleman said. "I was standing here, getting my bearings and trying to figure out which direction to turn so we could make a run for it, when everything illuminated. It was just for a second."

"Which direction did the light come from?" I asked.

They glanced at each other.

"Over where she's standing." Mack pointed at Fanny.

"As if someone had come in through the main tent entrance?" I asked.

"Yeah, that would work," Coleman said. "If they came in that way, they'd have a clear shot straight at Bathsheba."

That fit with the injury to Bathsheba's chest. The bolt of magic had been a direct hit from the front. Coleman and Mack would have had trouble finding their way in the pitch black to shoot Bathsheba so directly.

"You didn't see anyone standing in the entrance of the tent when the magic hit?" I asked.

"Nah. The light was so bright that I was dazzled," Mack said.

"Same here," Coleman said. "There was the whack of magic that hit Bathsheba, and then someone cried out. At which point, I'd figured my way out, grabbed Mack by the collar, and hauled him after me. We got out the back and were running for it when you caught us."

"Tempest, this is all very interesting," Dazielle said, "but we don't have much time."

"We don't need much more time." I walked to the entrance, turned, and extended my fingers, pointing them at Dazielle.

She flinched back in the seat. "What are you doing?"

"Checking my sight line." I aimed at her chest. An unexpected spark of magic shot from my fingers and slammed into the chair right next to Dazielle's head.

She yelped and jumped up. "You could have killed me."

I shook out my fingers. "Oops! That was an accident. I didn't mean to do that."

"Sure, you didn't." Dazielle glowered at me. "Why don't you take the place of Bathsheba and let me throw magic at you?"

"No! No! It must be the stone circle. Everyone's magic is messing up." I stared at my still sparking fingers. That was seriously weird. I hadn't even been thinking about casting a spell.

"Are you sure that was an accident?" Dazielle's wings fluttered out around her.

"A hundred percent. Sit back down. I'm working something out." I pointed my finger at Dazielle again.

She narrowed her eyes. "Just you try it. You won't catch me out a second time."

"Liam, move in front of the chair and attempt to fire a spell at Dazielle," I said.

"Oh, no. I barely perform magic," he said.

"You're not going to do any actual magic," Dazielle said. "I've already been shot at by Tempest."

"I missed you," I said.

"Barely," she said.

"Do something small," I said to Liam. "Something that won't leave a mark."

Liam rubbed the back of his neck. "I can think of something that might work."

"Great. Get ready to move on three," I said. "Don't stop, no matter what I do. One, two, three, go." I clicked my fingers and plunged the tent into darkness.

There were several gasps, then I heard a thud and a curse.

I sensed Liam moving around as a swish of air passed my face.

"What was that?" Dazielle yelped in the darkness. "Something hit me."

I clicked my fingers and returned light back into the tent.

Liam stood to the left of the gold chair, blinking his eyes. "I used a paint spell. I only ever mastered spells when I was a child."

"Getting by on your good looks, I imagine," Mack muttered.

Liam ran a hand through his hair and smirked. "I make no apologies for using my assets."

I looked over at Dazielle. She had a blob of red on the left leg of her white pants. If Liam had tried to kill Bathsheba, he'd have been way off with his shot unless he'd gotten really lucky.

Dazielle glared down at her ruined pants. "How am I supposed to get that out?"

"This is all in a good cause," I said. "It shows how hard it would have been for Liam to get around the chair and make a clean shot."

Liam rubbed his knee. "I slammed into the arm of that wretched thing as I walked around it. That'll leave a bruise."

I pointed my fingers at Dazielle again. "Was there a downward trajectory to the bolt that hit Bathsheba in the chest?"

Dazielle shook her head. "It was a straight shot."

"Which means that standing here, I'm too high up. I'd have needed to angle my magic downward to get the shot in the right place. Whoever shot Bathsheba was short."

All eyes swiveled to Fanny.

She backed away and bumped into an angel. "It wasn't me. I may be on the short side, but I didn't kill Bathsheba."

"Come stand over here in front of me," I said. "Aim at Dazielle. Point at her chest as if you were going to shoot her."

Fanny licked her lips. "What if this proves that I could have done it?"

"We're just testing a theory," I said. "Whoever killed Bathsheba has got to be under five feet tall."

"I am, but I still didn't do it." Fanny's hand shook as she pointed at Dazielle.

I edged her hand down. "Why are you aiming so high? If you fired from that angle, it would go straight over Dazielle's head. You're way off."

Fanny's cheeks grew pink. "My... eyesight's not what it used to be."

"Hold on a second. You're saying you can't see clearly from this distance?" I asked.

She gave a little shrug. "I've been told I need glasses or laser surgery. I've lived for so long with the world having a slightly fuzzy outline that I'm used to it. The haze makes everything seem so pretty."

"What does Dazielle looked like to you from this distance?" I asked.

"A beautiful blur of shimmering white," Fanny said.

I groaned. If I didn't already have doubts about Fanny, this ruled her out as the killer. She couldn't even see straight to shoot Bathsheba.

I stood behind her and sighted along her shaking arm. "Even if you did get in a lucky strike, you're still too high. Take off your heels and duck down a bit."

Fanny kicked off her shoes and bent her knees.

"That would just about do it," I said.

Fanny shrieked as a red jagged swirl of magic shot from the palm of her hand and set light to Dazielle's wing.

Dazielle leaped to her feet and flapped her wing in the air until the flames were extinguished.

"Oh my gosh! I'm so sorry." Fanny lowered her hand and stared at her palm. "That wasn't meant to happen. I don't—"

"Let me guess. The stone circle made you do it." Dazielle inspected the charred feathers on her wing.

"That must be it," Fanny said. "I mean, I was focusing hard and thinking about killing you with magic, but that was all I was doing."

"I feel so much better knowing that," Dazielle muttered.

I pressed my lips together to stop from smiling. The stone circle was having fun with Dazielle.

"What about you two?" I looked over at Coleman and Mack.

"You can count me out," Mack said. "I'm over six feet tall."

"Not when you kneel," I said.

He scrubbed the stubble on his chin. "That's not happening. My knees are ruined. It's way too painful for me to kneel for long."

"Coleman?" I asked.

He shook his head. "It wasn't me either. It would have been impossible to get around the chair without whacking into it. That would have given the game away. All I was interested in was making a run for it."

I nodded. I'd been thinking the exact same thing. My gaze slid to Charlotte and Picasso, who were sitting together quietly.

I kneeled beside their seats and aimed at Dazielle again.

My breath caught in my throat. This was the perfect position to hit Bathsheba.

I stood and stared down at them. "So, which one of you did it? Who fired the spell that killed your mom?"

Chapter 19

Nobody spoke for several seconds. The tension grew inside the tent, and it seemed that even the stone circle was listening for an answer.

"We had nothing to do with this," Picasso said. "I was injured by Mom's killer. I'd hardly do that to myself."

"You received a flesh wound," I said, "which you said was easily healed. Maybe you inflicted an injury on yourself to make it look like you were a victim, so no one would consider you as the killer."

"You're suggesting I blasted a spell at my own arm after I'd killed my mom?" He shook his head. "You have no idea what you're talking about."

I glanced at Dazielle, and she nodded at me to continue. "Did you act alone, or was Charlotte also involved?"

"Don't say a word," Charlotte said. "This witch knows nothing."

A muscle in Picasso's jaw tightened as he looked away.

"I take that to mean she was involved. Did you kill Bathsheba for the money?" I said.

Picasso lowered his head. "Bathsheba was a monster."

"Don't!" Charlotte grabbed his hand. "This has nothing to do with anybody else. This is our family business."

"Everyone should know the real truth about the famous Bathsheba Delaware," Picasso said. "She was cold, cruel, and spiteful. She didn't love us. She used us."

I nodded slowly. "To make herself look better. She adopted you to improve her public image. The famous singer with the caring side, taking on two abandoned children."

Liam cleared his throat. "Bathsheba had her moments. She was an artist. She was always highly strung. That could make her difficult to be around but not cruel."

"I've met plenty of artists while I've worked for her," Charlotte said. "None of them behaved like she did."

"What did she do to you that was so bad?" I asked.

Neither of them spoke for several seconds.

"Charlotte used to be a singer," Picasso said.

"Quit talking," Charlotte hissed at him. "That doesn't matter."

"It does. She'd often sing with Mom when she was little. Mom used to find it cute. She'd even encourage her."

Charlotte sighed. "Then my talent grew. All those hours of singing paid off. That's when Mom turned nasty."

"Bathsheba saw you as competition?" I said.

"She pretended she didn't mind," Charlotte said. "But I could tell she didn't approve of how good I was getting. She used to bring me out at the end of concerts and we'd perform together. The crowd would cheer and clap us on. Suddenly, she stopped doing that. And then one night, she..." She shook her head and looked at her clasped hands.

"Mom gave Charlotte a drink. She said it would make her sound even better."

Fanny gasped. "She did the same thing to me. She ruined my ability to sing for weeks."

"Lucky you. My singing voice was taken for good." Charlotte's lips thinned. "Mom told me it was a magic cocoa. I was so surprised by her kindness that I drank it down, despite it tasting bitter. I was only fifteen at the time and thought my mom would never do anything bad to me. I should have known better. I'd seen her evil side plenty of times."

"You couldn't sing after you drank that?" I asked.

"My singing voice was gone," Charlotte said. "I couldn't speak for almost a month, and when I finally got my voice back, it was different. Every time I sing now, I feel pain. Mom did that because she hated anyone being better than her."

"That's terrible. I always knew she was spiteful and fearful of anyone else with talent," Fanny said, "but I had no idea about this. Why didn't you leave her?"

"We thought about it plenty of times," Picasso said. "We used to stay up late and sneak into each other's rooms and discuss how we were going to do it. After Mom punished me for taking a cookie without asking, I even ran away."

"He came back because of me." Charlotte shook her head.

"Of course. I couldn't bear the thought of you being alone with that monster."

I looked over at Liam. "You let this happen? Did you see Bathsheba being cruel to her children?"

He raked a hand through his hair. "I've not always been there. We only married recently."

"You saw enough to know she wasn't a natural mother." Charlotte sneered at him. "You just chose to look the other way, so your privileges wouldn't get taken away. None of her previous husbands lifted a finger to stop her, though. They didn't care about us. They were only in it for the money."

"Wait now. That's not true," Liam said. "I did mention her behavior once or twice, but everyone knows what Bathsheba was like. She warned me to keep quiet. I was simply the airhead husband. If I'd said anything bad about her, it would only look like I was trying to build public sympathy for myself."

"You could have done something," I said, "anything, if she was being abusive to people in her care."

His shoulders sagged as he glanced at Charlotte and Picasso. "Maybe I could have done more."

Picasso shook his head. "She mistreated you the same as us. You had your own problems to sort through."

"I understand why you didn't feel able to stay when you were younger, but why not leave now?" I asked. "You're both grown up."

"That's what we'd planned on doing," Picasso said. "As soon as our trust funds kicked in, there'd be no reason for us to stay."

"That was until Mom started talking about adopting another child," Charlotte said.

My eyes widened. "You didn't want her to go through with this adoption?"

"Of course not!" Charlotte threw her hands up. "We couldn't allow another child to suffer like we have. It was so wrong. Mom was allowed to adopt us and parade us around like the gems she hung about her neck. We were just trophies to her perfect life. She barely spoke to us when we were out of the public eye. If we made any noise, she'd send us to our rooms without feeding us. She didn't care if we lived or died. She once left us alone in the house for a week. We were eight years old and terrified."

"We had to stop that from happening to anyone else," Picasso said. "We had to save Lucy, the girl Mom was planning to adopt."

I wasn't sure what to say. A part of me felt sorry for Charlotte and Picasso. They'd been trying to protect an innocent child from their vicious mother, but they didn't have to murder her to do it.

"I don't believe you," Liam blurted out. "What about the will?"

"What are you talking about?" I asked.

"In Bathsheba's will, she had a clear caveat. If a family member was charged with killing her, her money automatically went to a charitable foundation to immortalize Bathsheba. Every penny would be spent on statues, memorial gardens, and other permanent features all dedicated to her memory. We wouldn't get anything."

My gaze went to Mack and Coleman, who stood at the back of the tent shifting from foot to foot. They looked like they wanted to be anywhere but here. "Charlotte and Picasso hired you and set this up, so they'd get to keep their inheritance. Did you know it was them who contacted you to arrange the robbery?"

Mack raised a hand. "No, it was all done anonymously."

"It's a clever setup," I said. "It was easy to believe this was a robbery gone wrong."

"We don't care about the money," Charlotte said.

"Which is why you stayed until you got your trust funds," I said. "If things had been that awful, you would have left."

"This was all about Lucy and keeping her safe," Picasso said. "We'd rather she stay in care than become a part of this twisted family. Being adopted by Bathsheba has ruined us. If it wasn't for Charlotte, I wouldn't have survived."

I wasn't sure what to believe. Had they acted selflessly, killing their mom so they could protect this child, or was the motive greed and a desire to get their hands on their mom's wealth the major factor? The angels would have to figure that out.

"Tempest!" Dazielle pointed behind me.

I turned. The fog was creeping in under the tent entrance. The angels outside must have been overcome. We were almost out of time.

From the way Charlotte and Picasso were seated, Charlotte must have administered the killing blow to their mom. She was seated to Picasso's left and could easily have struck his arm with a non-fatal blow, making it look like they were innocent bystanders.

And it had worked. The injury on Picasso's arm had deflected my attention from him.

Dazielle stood and fluttered her wings. "We can run tests on your magic abilities if you don't confess. One of you did it."

"It was me." Picasso stood. "Charlotte has nothing to do with this. She tried to talk me out of it, but this was the only way I could see of getting out of this awful family, keeping Lucy safe, and getting our hands on Mom's money."

Charlotte jumped up and grabbed his hand. "No! You're not going down for this. I shot Mom. She deserved it. And it was easy for me. I know the layout of this tent. Mom was always so exacting where she wanted her chair placed. It wasn't a challenge to point and shoot from my seat."

Picasso turned to her. "You helped me when my life was difficult. You even stood in front of Bathsheba when she was coming after me and kept me safe. It's my turn to do the same for you."

Charlotte's eyes filled with tears as she shook her head. "I won't let you. She deserved this."

"You're both in trouble," Dazielle said. "Charlotte and Picasso Delaware, I'm arresting you for the murder of Bathsheba Delaware." She gestured to the two angels standing by the door.

They hurried over and stood on either side of Picasso and Charlotte.

An angel dashed into the tent outside. "It's lifting! The fog is retreating back inside the stone circle."

I blew out a relieved breath. We'd done it. We'd found out who really killed Bathsheba.

Dazielle strode over and gripped my shoulder. "Just so you know, it'll take me a while to forget that you blasted me with a spell."

"And here I was expecting a thank you." I stepped back. "And that was an accident. If I'd meant to hit you, I wouldn't have missed."

She smirked before her attention turned to the angels guarding Picasso and Charlotte. "Take them to the station for processing."

Mack and Coleman were also escorted out by other angels.

Fanny looked around and let out a sigh. "So, it's all over? I'm free to go?"

"It looks like you are." I shot a glance at Liam, who looked equal measures of confused and angry. "What are you going to do next?"

"Take a long hot soak in the tub and forget I ever visited Willow Tree Falls." Fanny finger waved me goodbye before disappearing out of the tent flap.

I glanced at Liam. "And you?"

"Get better judgment when it comes to women." His gaze tracked to the tent entrance.

"Fanny might take you back if you beg hard enough," I said. "There's no harm in asking for another chance."

"She's an incredible woman," he said. "I really would like to get to know her better without the terrifying threat of Bathsheba looming over us."

"Then go after her." I lifted my gaze to the top of the tent as he dashed out, calling after Fanny. It might not be a match made in heaven, but if it suited them, then there was nothing wrong with it.

I stepped out of the tent with Wiggles and stared at the stone circle. Everything felt calm. No magic crackled around the stones, the tension in the air had lifted, and there was no sign of the toxic fog.

"We did it again," he said.

"We always do," I said. "Let's hustle. We need to check everyone in the crypt is okay. Then I've got somewhere I need to be."

Chapter 20

"Will you just let go!" I tugged on the hem of my jeans, which was trapped between Wiggles' teeth.

"I'm mop betting goo eave." He growled and tried to drag me closer.

"Why are you talking about mops and goo?" I shook my leg. "Quit it."

He dropped his hold and backed away a few steps, his red eyes gleaming. "I was saying that I'm not letting you leave. I may be an awesome hellhound, but I can't feed myself."

"You won't have to. I've left instructions for Aurora to find. You have two choices. You can stay at the apartment and she'll drop by to feed you and walk you twice a day, or you can stay with her and Bandit."

"Ugh! I'm not sharing the same air with that deranged fairy cat," he said. "Do you really have to go?"

"You know I do." I adjusted the holdall on my shoulder and smoothed a hand over my newly restored black hair. "Finding Dad is the most important thing to me. I've been distracted for long enough. Difficult singers, lying children, cheating husbands! No more. I'm out of here to solve my own mystery."

We'd been over this half a dozen times since we'd left the stone circle the previous night. It had been too late to leave straight away after checking my family had recovered from their toxic fog encounter. I'd spent a couple of hours with them, giving them an update and making sure the prison was secure. Then I'd grabbed some sleep and was set for an early departure from the village just as the sun broke over the horizon.

The magic barrier beside me hummed contentedly, no longer shaking or sparking like it had been over the last few days.

Wiggles huffed out a cloud of smoke. "There's no guarantee Aurora will remember to feed me. You know what she's like when she has a new boyfriend. Plus, she has her special fairy friend to focus on. I'll be a distant memory."

"Aurora would never forget about you," I said. "She'll spoil you rotten. When I come back, I bet you'll be ten pounds heavier and have half a dozen new bow ties."

He grumbled under his breath. "She doesn't even know what my favorite treats are."

"She does! Anything sweet," I said.

"Maybe she won't walk me the right way. What if she insists I wear a harness or makes me walk with Bandit? Think of the humiliation." He shook his head.

"This is Aurora we're talking about. She'll bend over backward to make sure you're happy." I knelt and scratched behind his ears with my nails. "I'll miss you too. I won't be long. You never know, if all goes well, I could be at Puzzlewood and back again before the end of the day."

"I never said I'd miss you. This way, at least I get to have the bed all to myself. And your pillows. The plans I have for them." Wiggles leaned against my hand for a second.

I narrowed my eyes. "Stay away from the pillows, or I'll send you to doggy boarding with Abigail."

His nose wrinkled. "If you do that, I'll be the one leaving home."

"Abigail would take great care of you. And she has that amazing grooming parlor set up out back. She might even dye you, so you turn puce again. And I bet if you asked really nicely—"

"No grooming or dying of fur! I'm happy to be back to sexy tan brown."

"Then no defiling my pillows."

He grunted. "I'll think about it."

I stood. "I need to get a move on."

Wiggles peered up at me, his furry brow wrinkling. "You know, if your dad returning to Willow Tree Falls was easy, don't you think he'd have come back by himself? Any magic user can find the village if they want to."

I ignored the nervous flutter in my stomach. "Maybe it's not so easy for him. He could be worried that he's been away for so long that we've all forgotten about him. And, there is, of course, the Frank issue." I nudged Frank inside my head to see if he had anything to say about the matter, but he refused to comment. Typical stubborn demon. But I was close to the truth. I just knew it.

"I'm just saying," Wiggles gave his version of a shrug, "it might not all be moonlight and roses when you reunite."

I swallowed around the growing lump in my throat. "Yeah, I've not thought about much else in months. But, one way or the other, I have to know why he left us."

Wiggles was silent for several seconds as he kicked under his armpit with a back paw. "What if Aurora insists on giving me a nightly bath? You know how that ginger fur ball of hers insists on highly scented and unpleasant smelling bubble baths."

"You might enjoy sharing a bath with Bandit."

"I'd rather shave off all my fur."

I chuckled. "Aurora knows you like to roll around in foul-smelling things from time to time. If you promise you won't roll around in anything gross, perhaps she won't bathe you."

"But what about—"

"No more stalling. I wish you could come with me." I didn't want to do this on my own, but it was the easiest way.

He huffed again. "I know, if I step outside the magical barrier, all my hellhound awesomeness vanishes. I end up squished on the ground, a lifeless pile of handsome fur."

"Exactly. I'll be back before you know it. You keep an eye on things until I return. Let me know about all the dumb stuff the angels have done in my absence. At least they'll be happy Oriel is awake."

"I'll keep a tally."

"Where do you think you're going?"

I turned to see Tilly Machello standing with her arms crossed over her chest.

"Um, hi! Long-time no see."

She arched an eyebrow. "I've almost forgotten what you look like. What's going on here?"

"Same old, same old." I grimaced. I hadn't intentionally let our friendship slide, but if I wasn't demon hunting, I was chasing after the angels and trying to sort out their mess. It left me little time for much else.

"You have a bag packed, and it looks like you're saying goodbye to the fuzz ball."

My mouth twisted to the side. "I've been a bad friend."

"You've been a terrible friend," she said. "You missed all the dinners I invited you to, including the one where I made the seven-layer lasagna with triple cheese." She strode closer, her gaze traveling over me, taking in the holdall slung over one shoulder.

"I'd have come if I'd known there'd be triple cheese." I sounded as lame as I felt.

"So, what's going on?" Tilly asked. "This isn't about the stone circle, is it? I heard you were involved with the problems there. Of course, if you talked to me once in a while, I wouldn't have to listen to village gossip to find out what you were up to."

"I really am sorry about that."

She waved a hand in the air. "Fill me in now. Have you got time for coffee and a muffin?"

"I wish I had," I said.

Tilly sighed. "I get it. Too busy saving the world to worry about your old friend."

"Don't say that." I took a step toward her. "When I get back, I promise I'll take you out to dinner every night of the week. My treat."

"You do know that I own the best restaurant in Willow Tree Falls, right?" She shook her head, the glimmer of a smile on her face. "But dinner would be nice. And I'm guessing, since the stone circle has quietened down, you've solved whatever that problem was."

"Pretty much. The stones were grouching because the angels had arrested the wrong person for Bathsheba Delaware's murder."

"I've heard a different name mentioned every day in connection to that murder. The last I heard, it was the other singer. I saw her perform. She was incredible."

"It wasn't her. Nor was it the guys who robbed Bathsheba after the concert."

"Who I happened to spot and bring down before they could escape." Wiggles puffed out his chest.

Tilly petted his head. "Of course, you did. So, if it wasn't the other singer or the robbers, who was it?"

"Bathsheba's adopted children, Charlotte and Picasso," I said. "They got sick of being treated like accessories to be used by Bathsheba to make her popular. And when she decided to adopt another girl, they snapped. Muddled in with that is a lot of money they were due to inherit. With Bathsheba dead, her children would have received the bulk of her enormous fortune."

Tilly whistled. "Not anymore."

"You got that right. Bathsheba must have figured out that her family weren't that keen on her. There was a caveat in her will stating that, if any family member murdered her, the money goes to charity to immortalize Bathsheba in statues and memorial gardens. All tacky sounding stuff. I hope there are no plans to have a statue of her in the village."

"Wow! No wonder you've been busy. So much for family loyalty."

"It took me a while to work this one out," I said. "Bathsheba was so unpopular that everyone in her life wished her dead."

"And the stone circle was grumpy because it wanted the right person charged with murder?"

"Bathsheba's murder took place within twenty paces of the stones. That made it angry. It wanted to see justice done."

"Good for the stone circle. I just wish it hadn't made such a mess of the village."

"Are you having problems in the restaurant?"

"Not anymore. The floor is no longer creaking under my feet, and the food isn't coming out burned, so I'm happy," Tilly said. "Now, do you want to talk about this other business that's making you leave so sneakily?"

"Not just yet. I'm hoping it'll all be explained soon enough. But I need to get somewhere quickly."

"Wait up!"

I glanced over Tilly's shoulder. Aurora, Granny Dottie, and Bandit in cat form were racing toward me.

This was the last thing I needed. I'd planned to slip out of the village quietly, head to Puzzlewood, and see what I could find out. My secret mission had just been blown wide open.

"You're going without us?" Aurora arrived first, her cheeks pink and her newly restored blonde hair a fuzzy mess around her head as if she'd just rolled out of bed.

Granny Dottie was still in her house slippers and hair rollers. Yep, this had been an emergency dash to try to stop me from leaving.

I rubbed the back of my neck as I looked at the unhappy expressions on their faces. "No. Well, I didn't want to tell you what I was doing in case nothing came of it. You'd have only gotten your hopes up. This might all be for nothing."

"I have to come with you," Aurora said. "He's my dad too!"

I grabbed her shoulder and squeezed. "Of course. I get that. But what if he's... different?"

Granny Dottie tutted. "Of course, he'll be different. He's been missing for years. We've all changed during that time. But he'll still be your father."

"I want to come with you," Aurora said.

My protective big sister urge took over, and I shook my head as I clutched her shoulder. "Stay here. There's a lot to sort out after the stone circle's misbehavior. People need you around to restore order. There's lots of damage to the stores, yours included. And people might need help to fix up their homes. You're great at that kind of magic."

"Uh uh. You can't get rid of me that easily," Aurora said. "My store is behaving impeccably now the stone circle is happy again. Any tidying up can wait. I can take a few days off and join you."

I glanced at Granny Dottie. She raised her eyebrows before pursing her lips and turning to Aurora. "Your sister's right. You stay here. The family needs you. We're going to have to do some preparation for when Tempest brings your dad back. It's going to be a shock to us all."

I glanced at Tilly, who was taking this all in. She caught my eye and nodded, a glimmer of sympathy on her face. She realized what a huge deal this was for me.

Aurora tugged on her bottom lip. "I didn't think about that. Everyone will be happy to see Dad again, won't they?"

"I'm sure we'll all be delighted once we've gotten over the shock," Granny Dottie said. "Think of your mom. She hasn't seen him for a long time. Cora's a strong woman, but this will take some getting used to. We need to break it to her gently, get her used to the idea. I expect she'll have a lot of questions. And she might also not be happy with the two of you for keeping this a secret. We need to soften her up."

"We kept it a secret because she'd have only worried if we'd told her everything we'd learned," I said.

"I know that. You did this for her own good and everyone else's." Granny Dottie walked over and tucked her hand in mine. "Tempest, you can't protect everybody from the bad things that happen in this world. Cora will accept this, but she'll need her family around her to do it. Aurora stays here and helps, while you go bring your father home."

I hoped my gaze conveyed my gratitude to Granny Dottie. For all her ditziness, she understood that it was better if Aurora stayed here.

I didn't want things going wrong when I arrived to find our dad. Granny Dottie was right. He could have changed. He might not be the man I remembered.

And it was more than that. When I faced him, it had to be alone. I had to know if a deal had been made with Frank and if part of that deal was my dad leaving the village. I hadn't yet figured out how to get around that if it was true.

"How about this for a compromise if you're worried about Tempest's safety?" Bandit backed up, shook her fur out, and transformed into a glorious, green shimmering fairy. "I'll come with you."

"Wow! That cat's a fairy." Tilly took a step back, her eyes wide. "That's not something you see every day."

"I have so much I need to tell you," I said.

"And you will, right after you get back from dealing with this." She gave me a nod and a wink. Things were good between us, but I was still taking Tilly out for a blowout feast when I got back. Good friends were hard to find.

I stared up at Bandit, noting her sparkling eyes and sharp teeth. "You really want to be my traveling buddy?"

"No! You can't take her," Wiggles said.

"Are you jealous, furball?" Bandit extended a sparkling wing and showered him in glitter.

He shook out his fur. "Ouch! That stings."

"I can do a lot more than simply sting," Bandit said. "Now I have my abilities back, you may find me useful. Tempest, I'm offering you my services."

I tilted my head as I considered the offer. It wouldn't be the worst thing to have a huge, powerful fairy on my side. That was if Bandit was on my side. Could I trust her? She was tied into my dad's mystery. Somehow, she'd known he was alive and had come to the village with a message for us. Where had that message originated from?

Aurora shot me a worried look. "I don't like the idea of Bandit going too."

Bandit swept Aurora into her wings. "I've been trapped as a cat in this tiny village for far too long. I need to spread my wings, in the literal and figurative sense. I've never stayed in one place for long. It's time for a new adventure."

Aurora sighed and rested her head on Bandit's glittering chest. "You're leaving me?"

Bandit lowered Aurora to the ground and ducked until she was eye level with her. She curled a wing around her back and pulled her close. "You're the sweetest witch I've ever had the pleasure to meet. And although at times, I was almost suffocated to death by your kindness, it made me see that sometimes you can solve things without violence."

Aurora glanced over her shoulder at me before placing a hand on Bandit's broad, shimmering chest. "That's good to know. I've loved having you here. The store won't be the same without you. I've come to rely on you. I'll... I'll miss you."

Bandit placed a kiss on Aurora's forehead, leaving behind a smear of multi-colored shimmer. "You took me in when no one else would. When I was weak and had been turned into a pointless bundle of fur with next to no magic abilities—"

"And a bad attitude," Wiggles said.

Bandit glared at him. "That's my usual attitude. As I was saying, Aurora, you gave me a home. You showered me in affection and believed in me when no one else did. I will forever be in your debt, Aurora Crypt. I will protect you with my life should the need ever arise. A fairy doesn't say those words lightly."

My eyebrows shot up. It was no small thing for a fairy to pledge herself to you. Aurora had made a powerful ally, albeit one who was less than stable and obsessed with glitter.

Aurora ducked her head and sniffed. "I'll keep a bed for you in case you change your mind or want to visit for a weekend."

"Cat-sized or fairy-sized bed?" Bandit expanded her wings, shrouding us in shadow.

"Whatever size you want." Aurora rested her head briefly against Bandit's chest again. "I wish you would stay."

Wiggles loudly cleared his throat. "In case you hadn't noticed, I'm not going anywhere."

Aurora swiped at her eyes and smiled at him. "Of course. We can keep each other company while they're gone."

"And you'll be pleased to know I'm leaving behind all my scented bath oils," Bandit said as she released Aurora from her wing. "I suggest you get used to using them, you stinking hound."

"I won't miss you," Wiggles said. "You've been nothing but a big pain in my furry behind since you walked into Willow Tree Falls and started finding bodies."

"Trust me, the feeling is very mutual." Bandit flipped Wiggles off the ground with a wing and caught him in the air before planting a big kiss on his muzzle.

Wiggles squirmed several times before he licked her cheek. "I haven't enjoyed a moment of our time together."

Bandit roared a laugh. "The same here, furball."

Aurora eased Wiggles out of Bandit's grip. "Make sure you look out for Tempest. She's prone to bouts of ridiculousness. She throws herself into danger without thinking about it and always waits until she's too hungry before she eats. That makes her grouchy."

"I do neither of those things," I said.

"You do too," Aurora said. She wrapped an arm around my waist. "Which is why we all love you so much. It's a good idea if Bandit goes with you."

"I can do this on my own," I said.

"Yes, we all know what a strong, independent witch you are," Granny Dottie said. "Thanks to you, the stone circle is happy again, and the village is safe. But asking for a little help now and again isn't a sign of weakness. Take the enormous sparkling fairy with you. She'll be an asset."

Bandit inclined her head at Granny Dottie. "Indeed, I will. And I don't lend my services out easily. Be grateful for them."

I studied Bandit as she teased Wiggles and threatened him with a glitter bomb. I definitely could do with some backup while I headed to Puzzlewood. It was generally a safe place, but I haven't been there for years, and it could take a while to find my dad. Having the services of a fairy, who would most likely intimidate the heck out of a lot of people, could be useful.

"Don't forget our dinner date when you get back," Tilly said. "We have a lot of catching up to do."

"I won't stand you up again," I said.

Once this was over, I was taking a long break from any mysteries. I'd run Cloven Hoof, sleep in late, and hang out with my guy, my friends, and my family. That was it.

"Okay, I'll take Bandit with me. Everyone else stay here and clear up after the stone circle's hissy fit," I said.

Aurora sighed but nodded. "Be careful. No one knows what you're going to find out there."

Granny Dottie patted my arm. "Whatever you find, stay safe. Don't do anything risky."

"I can't guarantee that," I said. I was willing to risk a lot to have this mystery solved once and for all. "We're so close to finding Dad."

A nervous smile flickered across Aurora's face. She leaned closer until her mouth was by my ear. "And keep an eye on Bandit. In her fairy form, she can be a bit... unpredictable."

"I can hear you," Bandit said.

Aurora jerked back and grinned at her. "I'm only telling the truth."

"Sometimes, you're too truthful for your own good." Bandit glowered at her. "It's a good job I like you and you have my unwavering gratitude."

Aurora raced over and hugged Bandit, who looked down at her with an amused gleam in her eyes as she petted her head.

I took a look around the group as I stepped to the edge of the magic barrier. Everyone was supporting me in this mission. Now that Willow Tree Falls was back to normal, I could leave and finally finish what I started.

Nervous excitement fluttered through me as Bandit came to stand by my side.

"Are you ready to do this, witch?" She yawned and stretched out her wings.

"Let's do it." I nodded as I waved goodbye to everyone. Life was about to change. Our dad was coming home. All the questions I had about what happened to him were about to be answered.

"How about we fly?" Bandit grabbed my hand before I had a chance to answer and yanked me into the air.

I gulped and looked down at the ground that already seemed far from my feet. Yep, life was about to become very different. I had to hope we were all ready for it.

About Author

K.E. O'Connor (Karen) is a cozy mystery author living in the beautiful British countryside. She loves all things mystery, animals, and cake. When she's not writing about mysteries, murder, and treats, she volunteers at a local animal sanctuary, reads a ton of books, binge watches mystery series, and dreams about living somewhere warmer.

To stay in touch with the fun mysteries:

Newsletter:
www.subscribepage.com/cozymysteries

Website:
www.keoconnor.com

Facebook:
www.facebook.com/keoconnorauthor

Also By

Luck of the Witch
Hell of a Witch
Revenge of the Witch
Curse of the Witch
Son of a Witch
Framing of the Witch
Trickery of the Witch
Wishes of the Witch
Harmony of the Witch
Remedy of the Witch
Gift of the Witch
Toil of the Witch
Jinxing of the Witch
Craving of the Witch
Union of the Witch
Chaos of the Witch
Sleighing of the Witch

If you enjoyed

Harmony of the Witch

turn the page to read an extract from the next Crypt
Witch Mystery

REMEDY OF THE WITCH

Chapter 1

I stuffed the plump, lavender scented pillow over my head to drown out the bickering that had been raging for five minutes.

"She's always liked me better than you," Bandit said. "That's why Tempest brought me here and left your chunky behind in Willow Tree Falls."

"That's not true," Wiggles said on the other end of the snow globe. "You know I can't leave the village."

"That's an excuse," Bandit said. "If Tempest wanted you in Puzzlewood, you'd be here."

I groaned and hurled the pillow at Bandit. "Quit teasing my hellhound. He's right. He can't leave Willow Tree Falls."

Bandit sat on the edge of her bed in the motel room we were using as our temporary base, a gleeful look on her sparkly face. "A fairy never lies. I'm here because you like me the best."

"Tempest, tell me that's not true." A note of anxiety threaded through Wiggles' words as his nose loomed large in the snow globe.

"I'm insulted you even have to ask that question," I said. "You know I'd have brought you with me if I could."

Since we'd arrived in Puzzlewood on the hunt for my dad less than twenty-four hours ago, Wiggles had been messaging at every opportunity.

Not that I minded him getting in touch. It was sweet that he missed me. But it was inconvenient, especially when I needed to be laser-focused on tracking down Dad and not worrying about what was going on back home.

The thought of finding my dad sent a shiver of anticipation through me. I hadn't seen him for years. It felt like I was on the cusp of something momentous that would affect the whole family. Our lives were about to change if this worked out.

"I hope you're looking after Tempest properly," Wiggles said.

"I can look after myself just fine." I slid off the silky comforter on my deluxe bed and walked over to the table.

We'd checked into what I'd figured was a basic motel, but I'd been surprised by the luxury. And the staff had bent over backward to accommodate us. They hadn't blinked an eye at the enormous fairy accompanying me, who shed glitter wherever she went.

"Aurora wanted me to ask if you're eating properly," Wiggles said.

"We left the village a day ago. I can't have become malnourished in that short amount of time."

Wiggles sniffed. "You must at least be hungry."

I shrugged. "I could definitely eat." My fingers traced over the hard wood table that was set with a platter of treats.

I'd forgotten how great Puzzlewood was. We used to vacation here years ago. Back then, I'd seen it through a child's eyes, all the fun things to do and the great tasting food to stuff down, but this place had some seriously amazing luxury for the adults too.

I plucked a complimentary chocolate off the table and popped it into my mouth.

"Hey! What are you eating?" Wiggles asked.

"Only the finest chocolate you're never going to taste," Bandit said. "And we're not bringing any back for you if you keep pestering us."

"Of course, we are." I turned to the snow globe. "How's everything back home?"

Wiggles' red eyes glowed for a second as I chewed the chocolate. "Granny Dottie and Aurora haven't worked up the courage to tell your mom what's going on."

I blew out a breath, an unwelcome throb of tension in my shoulders. I was glad I'd left them to break the news to the rest of the family about this mission. It wasn't the bravest move on my part, but Mom would have panicked, flapped around, and then insisted she come with me.

I needed to check things out before anyone else got involved. Dad had been gone a long time, and as much as I tried to fool myself, he'd be a different man from the one I remembered.

"Make sure you prod them into action before too long," I said. "And don't let Granny Dottie anywhere near the brandy before she's revealed what's going on. She needs a clear head when this news comes out."

"It's too late for that," Wiggles said. "She was sneaking the stuff into her morning oatmeal. What are you going to do now you're there?"

I wrinkled my nose. "Take a look around. See if anyone's seen Dad. Get his picture out there. Maybe he'll hear that we're looking for him and come find us."

"And then we're going to enjoy the facilities at Puzzlewood," Bandit said. "They have a water park. No one told me about that. I'd have brought my rubber ring."

"We're not here for fun," I said. "This isn't a vacation. Let's not get distracted." I pushed aside the brochure about the water park Bandit offered me.

"One tiny hour enjoying ourselves won't hurt anyone," Bandit said. "It'll be fun."

"You can't go to the water park with her," Wiggles said, a growl echoing through the snow globe and making it rattle.

"She can hardly take you," Bandit said. "You'd shed fur everywhere and make the water smell like rotten eggs with your sulfuric stink."

"I could wear a onesie bathing costume," Wiggles said. "It would be fine. Don't go to the water park with Bandit."

"No one's going to any water park," I said. "Wiggles, you concentrate on keeping the family together. Once word about this gets out, they'll be tricky to deal with."

"Of course. I won't let you down," he said.

"I'm bored. And we need to get more food," Bandit said. "Flying always makes me hungry. And I was carrying extra weight."

Bandit had flown us to Puzzlewood in record time. My stomach still wasn't settled from the bumpy journey, but it had been a quick way to get here. Plus, I'd been concentrating so hard on not being ill that I'd not had time to worry that I was about to find my dad after all this time.

"Stick to salads and plain food," Wiggles said. "Don't go eating pizza together. Pizza is our food. Tempest, promise me you won't eat pizza with that sparkling beast."

Poor Wiggles. He hated that he wasn't with me. And I didn't like leaving him behind. But thanks to the magic I'd used to bring him back to life as a hellhound, he could never leave Willow Tree Falls. That left me stuck with one enormous, mildly deranged fairy as a sidekick. I still wasn't certain it was a great idea that Bandit was here with me.

"We'd better go," I said.

"Make sure you check in with me every hour," Wiggles said.

"I'll try for once a day. Take care of everyone back there." We said our goodbyes. I ended the connection and placed the snow globe back on the bedside table.

"So, food and then the water park?" Bandit stood and stretched her enormous wings, flapping them around and causing a small hurricane in the room.

"No! This place is big, and we've only been around a fraction of it since we arrived. We need to get the word out that we're looking for my dad."

"We still need to eat," Bandit said. "Those chocolates are great, but I need my fruits and veggies. I'll be five minutes. I'll go get some chips and dip for you and something yummy for me." She turned to the window and grunted. "I thought this place always had perfect weather."

"It does. It's one of the things people love about it. You can always guarantee sunshine."

"Not today, you can't." She strode to the window.

I joined her and stared at the huge hailstones that hammered down outside. "That's weird."

"Hail doesn't bother me," Bandit said. "I'll go grab the food."

Before I had a chance to protest that we were wasting time, she flung the door open and shot into the sky.

I slammed it shut to stop the hail from getting in and continued to stare out the window. People raced past, their hands covering their heads as they tried to dodge the hailstones that rained down on them. The hail was big enough to chip glass. There must be something off with the weather magic in Puzzlewood.

I stepped away from the window and turned to the mirror. I looked paler than usual, most likely due to my bad night of sleep yesterday. I smoothed my hands down my hair. What would Dad think of me after all this time? Would he even recognize me? I was about a foot taller and had filled out my gawky teenage frame, but other than that, I didn't look much different.

He couldn't have forgotten about us. He must have stayed away because it was best for the whole family. He'd always been a selfless guy, putting the family first. That had to be the reason he'd walked out.

I was certain that, once I found him, everything would be explained, and he'd be happy to come back to Willow Tree Falls. Back to the family he belonged in.

I patted my chest. "What do you think, Frank? Are you happy that I'm about to find my dad after all these years?"

My incumbent demon, Frank, had been refusing to communicate for months. I was worried that his lack of communication was connected to my dad's disappearance. Rumor had it that a deal had been made between Frank and my dad that involved him having to leave the village.

I couldn't believe that, but if Dad thought it was best for me and would keep the family safe, I bet he'd make any deal that was needed. Even with a sly, deceitful demon who loved to cause chaos.

Frank, as had become the norm, remained silent on the matter.

"I'll get the truth out of you soon enough," I said. "You're living on borrowed time."

The door swung open. Bandit swooped in with a bag of groceries and a large white box in her hands. "Brunch is served." She set everything down with a flourish.

I unpacked the food. There was an enormous bowl of salad for Bandit, six bags of chips, a range of dips, prepacked sandwiches and cakes, and inside the white box, a tray of chocolate brownies.

"This will keep us going the whole time we're here," I said.

"Not the way I eat, it won't." Bandit scooped up the salad in her hand and began to eat. "You're only allowed one brownie."

"How generous." I eyed the dozen chocolate chip brownies that tempted me to skip the rest of the food and dive straight into the dessert.

"I'm just giving you a friendly warning," Bandit said. "You take more than one, and I'll break your hand."

I glowered at her. She would as well. Bandit was ten times stronger than me, and her glitter came with a stinging side-effect. I was just grateful that she was indebted to Aurora for taking her in when she'd been turned into a cat. Otherwise, we wouldn't be friends.

We set to work on the food, and I settled back on my bed with my solitary brownie by my side and a large bag of cheesy chips and garlic dip.

Bandit stuffed down the salad in a couple of minutes and grabbed two brownies. "I've been meaning to talk to you about something."

"What's that?"

She stretched out a wing and examined it. "It's about your dad."

I leaned forward on the bed. "Did you see him when you went out?"

"Oh, no, nothing like that." Bandit glanced away. "It's about the message I was supposed to give you."

"I already know about the message. Dad sent you to Willow Tree Falls to let us know he was safe."

"You're exactly right." Bandit bobbled her head from side to side.

"And yet there's something you missed?"

"It's a minor thing. I may have been a bit tardy about passing on the message."

"How tardy are we talking?" Bandit had only shown up in Willow Tree Falls a few months ago.

"About ten years."

My brownie fell from my hand. "You were supposed to tell us that Dad was alive and safe as soon as he left Willow Tree Falls?"

"Correct. We met three weeks after he left. We got talking, and he asked for my help."

"What the heck were you doing all that time?"

"I got distracted. It's easy to do. This world is a fascinating place. Your dad gave me the message and told me where to find you. He paid me well, so I was happy to do it."

"You got... distracted?" My fingers flexed, and magic sparked out of them.

"There's no point in getting your panties in a knot," Bandit said. "I got to you in the end."

"After you fooled around for a decade, got turned into a cat, and forgot the message you were supposed to tell us."

"Eventually, I remembered what I was supposed to do," Bandit said. "I did an excellent job. And being a cat is a traumatic experience. The less important things had to take a back seat."

I jumped off the bed and stalked toward her. "We spent years wondering where Dad was. We didn't know if he was dead or alive." I jabbed a finger against her chest. "And all this time, you knew. You had a message and didn't bother to pass it on because you got side-tracked."

Bandit's wings fluttered around her. "You have to remember, fairies live for thousands of years. For me, a decade is a blink of the eye."

"Not for us. It was a horrible time for the family. It could have been avoided if you'd passed on the message when you were supposed to. Even if we hadn't been able to find him, for whatever reason, we'd have known he was okay."

"You're stressing about nothing. Besides, witches live a long time too," Bandit said. "And you know now, so everything is sorted."

"Everything is not sorted." Bandit had to be kidding if she thought she could get away with this.

"It's as good as. We're here. Your dad is almost within touching distance. No harm was done."

Occasionally, there were times when I wished I had access to Frank's demon power. I'd have loved nothing more than to slam this fairy into the ground. But she had vicious wings, killer glitter, and teeth that could shred metal. Still, the urge to punch her was rearing up.

However, I had one weapon I could use against her. One that she'd do anything to avoid. It may be petty, but I was angry.

"I'm telling Aurora about this."

"Oh! You don't need to trouble her." Worry flickered across Bandit's face. She had a serious gooey spot for my little sister.

I shook my head and made sure to look sad. "Aurora cares about you. She took you in when no one else was interested in you. She nursed you back to health when you got sick, and all this time, you were hiding an important bit of information from her. She won't be so fond of you when she finds out about this."

Bandit scooped a wing around me and crushed me to her chest. "There's no need to involve Aurora. I'm telling you now because, when we meet your dad, he may remember what happened between us. I don't want any secrets."

"I hope he remembers. I'm hoping he's as angry as I am." I struggled in the tight embrace she held me in. It felt like a steel vice had wrapped around me.

"I'm helping now." Bandit shuffled me closer. "Aurora doesn't need to know about this. I'm sorry if it caused you any inconvenience."

"Inconvenience!" I thumped her chest and sparked hot magic against her skin until she released me. "Wiggles is right. Fairies can never be trusted."

Her nostrils flared. "I'm trustworthy. As soon as I finish these brownies, we'll find your dad and make everything right. You'll be so happy to see him that you'll forget my tiny oversight."

I glared at her. "Don't count on it."

"Maybe another brownie will change your mind." Bandit held out a dark chocolate brownie.

"I thought you'd break my hand if I had more than one."

"This is a peace offering. You may have two, but no more, or the hand breaking promise comes into play."

"Keep it." I was so angry with her that I'd lost my appetite. Even the alluring brownies no longer held any appeal.

I had to focus on finding my dad. I'd deal with this deceitful fairy another time.

Remedy of the Witch is available in e-book and paperback.